ONE HUNDRED AND EIGHT MILES.

Jed lights the lantern next to my bed and I flatten out Pa's map across my quilt. Seeing his familiar handwriting gives me a jolt. He's neatly printed place names, numbers, lines, dots, X's and two squares, one marked Winchester, the other, *Home*. Oh and look what he's done! He's drawn a little cave with bats hanging from the ceiling. Beside it is the printed word—*Cavetown*.

I know I have to go.

"Here's the path." Jed points to a dotted line that winds over what looks like squiggles of mountains, past Cavetown and across the broad line of a river. Seems to me I could follow that dotted line just as well as Jed. Seems to me that men and boys aren't the only ones who can go off to see the elephant.

⚜

"Meticulous historical details enrich the plot."
—*The Horn Book*

"Facts about the war are interwoven and the often-fraught-with-peril journey concludes in a satisfying manner."
—*Kirkus Reviews*

OTHER BOOKS BY SALLY M. KEEHN

The First Horse I See

I Am Regina

Moon of Two Dark Horses

Anna Sunday

SALLY M. KEEHN

PUFFIN BOOKS

The New War Map: Part of Virginia & Pennsylvania—
published by B.B. Russel, 515 Washington St., Boston, 1863

PATRICIA LEE GAUCH, EDITOR

PUFFIN BOOKS
Published by Penguin Group
Penguin Young Readers Group,
345 Hudson Street, New York, New York 10014, U.S.A.
Penguin Books Ltd, 80 Strand, London WC2R ORL, England
Penguin Books Australia Ltd, 250 Camberwell Road, Camberwell, Victoria 3124, Australia
Penguin Books Canada Ltd, 10 Alcorn Avenue, Toronto, Ontario, Canada M4V 3B2
Penguin Books (N.Z.) Ltd, 182-190 Wairau Road, Auckland 10, New Zealand

First published in the United States of America by Philomel Books,
a division of Penguin Putnam Books for Young Readers, 2002
Published by Puffin Books, a division of Penguin Young Readers Group, 2004

1 3 5 7 9 10 8 6 4 2

THE LIBRARY OF CONGRESS HAS CATALOGED THE PHILOMEL BOOKS EDITION AS FOLLOWS:
Keehn, Sally M.
Anna Sunday / Sally Keehn.
p. cm.
Summary: In 1863 twelve-year-old Anna, disguised as a boy and accompanied
by her younger brother Jed, leaves their Pennsylvania home and makes the
difficult journey to join their wounded father in Winchester, Virginia,
where they find themselves in danger from Confederate troops.
ISBN: 0-399-23875-1 (hc)
1. United States—History—Civil War, 1861–1865—Juvenile fiction.
[United States—History—Civil War, 1861–1865—Fiction. 2. Sex role—Fiction.]
I. Title. PZ7.K2257 An 2002 [Fic]—dc21 2001050081

Puffin Books ISBN 0-14-240026-2

Printed in the United States of America

*For my trumpet playing husband, David,
who sparked my interest in the Civil War.*

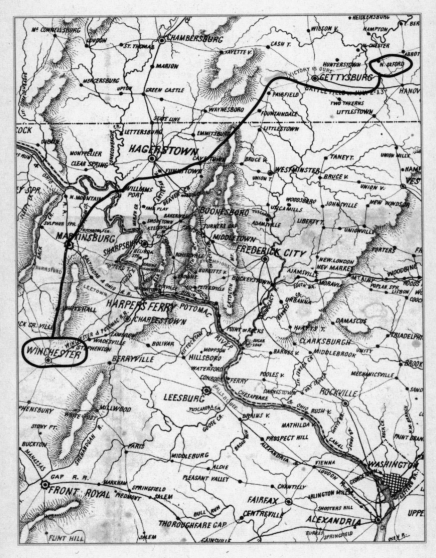

Anna's Journey

PART ONE

Leaving Home

ONE

I WISH MY PA WOULD come home to me today. I wish he'd swing me up and up until my flying feet hit the treetops! I hate it that he's gone!

I remember one day last August when Pa made a tiny boat out of scraps of oak wood—just for fun. He named the boat *Glory* in honor of our cousin Ezekiel. *"Glory! Glory hallelujah!"* Cousin Ezekiel loves to sing. Pa launched *Glory* in Conewago Creek and that little boat took off laughing. It bobbed down the rapids with all of us streaking along the creek bank after it—Pa, Cousin Ezekiel, my brother Jed and me. As our bobbing boat disappeared from view, Pa said, "Well look at that. *Glory's* off to see the elephant!"

Four months later, my dear pa went off to see the elephant, too. In a dark blue uniform the color of Cousin Ezekiel's eyes, Pa shouldered his musket and he left us to join the Union Army. He marched proudly past Butcher Frederick's Stand, out of New Oxford, Pennsylvania, and all the way to Winchester, Virginia, to meet up with the Eighty-seventh Regiment of Pennsylvania Volunteers. I stood in mud with December's gloomy clouds overhead and tried not to cry. A year ago last August, Sybil Freeman's pa went off to see the elephant. He never came back because a dirty Rebel shot and killed him at the Battle of Antietam. If my pa never came back, I don't know what I'd do.

"Is Pa's elephant Indian or African?" my little brother Jed, the great collector of facts, asks me. He's sprawled on the warm floor in front of our parlor fireplace. He's been collecting facts about elephants in one of Pa's old magazines while I darn socks. Outside the window, the April sky is elephant-gray and full of rain. Pa's been gone for over three long months.

"He didn't go off to see a real elephant, Jed. You know that. It's just an expression. It means going off to encounter something exciting, something you've never seen before. Like war. Like those dirty Rebels who want to tear apart our nation and destroy our homes." I hate those Rebels. I bite off my darning thread. One sock done.

"I bet Pa's elephant is African. African elephants are the fiercest," says Jed, who, as usual, has ignored what I've said. Jed's nine and he picks up facts as easy as a dog does fleas. Trouble with Jed is he chooses which facts he wants to believe and then twists them to fit into his way of thinking. Why, Jed likes to say our pa is President of the United States! It's because Pa and President Lincoln share the same first name—Abraham. People sing, "We are coming Father Abraham," and Jed gets all puffed up with pride.

"Anna." Jed stares out the window that overlooks our front yard with its white violets all in bloom. "It's Miss Bemis."

"Oh curses. Why today? She never comes on Fridays." I put aside my darning and hurry to the door. Ever since Pa headed south to see the elephant, our neighbor Miss Bemis has taken to calling on us, but only on Wednesdays and Saturdays. She often brings news of the war along with oatcakes, which, she claims, are good for our digestion. They just give us gas! She always brings her pokey nose—ready to sniff out problems we might have—living as we do without Pa, or Ma, who died three years back. As for the one adult in our household, Cousin Ezekiel, who had the misfortune of being dropped on his head when he was a baby and so he's just a little different, Miss Bemis says, "Ezekiel's simpleminded. He's nothing but a child with a beard! And so peculiar!"

I hate it when she says this. Cousin Ezekiel may be childlike, but in a good sense—loving, kind and he knows his Bible backward and forward. As for being peculiar, he just gets caught up in the glory of the Lord and has Holy Visions out in the field with his plow horse, Samson. Cousin Ezekiel says they see beautiful angels and archangels, which makes him forget about everyday things. Which is, when you think about it, quite understandable.

Now, trying to remember the manners I learned in *Mrs. Sloan's Book of Etiquette for Young Ladies* (which Pa gave me the day that I turned twelve), I swallow all curses and questions—*why today?*—and politely usher Miss Bemis into our parlor. I notice how she takes stock of my housekeeping and wish Jed could have been tidier with his magazines, which he's strewn all over the floor.

With her right foot, Miss Bemis sweeps aside *The 1863 Farmer's Almanac* so that she can stand in front of my neatly made fire, hog our heat and warm her broad backside. Pursing her lips, she brings out a letter from beneath her wet cloak. *A letter?* My stomach does a sickening somersault. News from the war comes in letters. Sometimes it's not happy news. I crane my neck to look at the handwriting. It's unfamiliar—squat and blocky.

"My nephew Stanley sent me this." Miss Bemis clears her throat and looks from Jed to me. "It's about your pa." She tries to make her expression somber, but a smile seems to tug at one corner of her mouth. Miss Bemis reads:

> Fort Milroy
> Winchester, Virginia
> March 30, 1863

My dearest aunt,

I have been meaning to write you for some time, but there are many interruptions to camp life, including the one I am writing you about. A week ago today, Abraham Sunday was shot while searching Rebel homes for contraband goods. A mini ball went through his right ankle. He refuses amputation & now pus has filled the joint & a dire infection has set in with chills and fever.

Pa's been shot?

6

We fear this is a mortal infection & he has asked me to relay to his two children & his cousin that he is thinking of them. He says to tell them that he dies having done his duty—giving his life for his country.

Pa's duty is to be with us! He can't die!

Please inform his family of this sad affair. I have commended our brother Abraham to God's good care. By the time you receive this note, he should be in God's heavenly kingdom, which, no doubt, is preferable to the she-devil's house in which he, because of his injured state, has been forced to stay. I remain—

Yours with deepest affection,
Stanley

My very heart stops beating. I look down at Jed. White-faced, he looks up at me. *Pa's been shot.* Rain pounds against our little house. Rain pours down our windowpanes. Miss Bemis says, "You can't stay on here without your pa. Not with that cousin of yours. You need to think—what do we do now?

"I know of a fine church home—Asylum for the Lambs. It takes in orphans of the war," she says as the front door opens and Cousin Ezekiel sweeps into the parlor with our dog, Anarchy. Cousin Ezekiel's long hair, gray beard and wet clothes drip water on the pinewood floor. Our cousin's dark blue eyes are bright and shining. His eyes fix on mine.

He brushes right past Miss Bemis. He doesn't realize

she's here! Doesn't know the contents of the letter she's holding! "There were wheels of fire and angels in the sky!" He's so excited he can barely speak. "Their singing filled the heavens! The wheels turned and burned, brighter, ever brighter. And in the midst of them appeared the Lamb!" He throws wide his arms.

The Lamb is Jesus Christ our comforter. Bursting into tears, I throw myself into Cousin Ezekiel's large warm arms. A sobbing Jed throws himself in beside me. Too caught up in his vision to notice that Jed and I are crying, Cousin Ezekiel just grabs us up and hugs us fiercely. His homespun shirt smells of his sweet plow horse, Samson.

Cousin Ezekiel slowly turns with us, round and round while he sings his favorite song—"The Battle Hymn of the Republic"—which he learned at a war rally last summer. *"Mine eyes have seen the glory of the coming of the Lord. . . ."* It was at that war rally Pa began to think he should go off to see the elephant. I remember.

Oh Pa. You never should have gone.

TWO

I LIKE TO THINK OF MY pa making bricks. My pa makes strong bricks from our New Oxford clay. That clay dries on his hands, turning them reddish-brown, the color of his beard. When Pa comes home from Mr. Alwine's brickyard, he lifts me up and swings me. Laughing, he rubs his soft-thick beard against my cheek. He calls me, "Anna, my apple dumpling queen." I call him, "Silly Pa. I love you, Pa."

Wish my pa could come home to me today. . . .

Jed, Cousin Ezekiel and I sit at our kitchen table, which Pa painted blue with chairs to match—just for fancy. The fried cornmeal mush and dandelion greens I fixed for supper sit untouched on our plates because we're all too upset to eat. A hard rain pelts our house. A hard rain beats against our windowpanes.

"No infection can kill your pa," Cousin Ezekiel says. He has finally come out of his Holy Vision and back into this dismal world where pas get shot by dirty Rebels and are forced to stay at a she-devil's house. "He'll get better."

"He'll come home. Pa *will* survive!" I find myself

shouting. Pa fills our house with his booming voice—"Anna, do I smell shoofly pie? Jed, shall we play checkers?" He paints our furniture in such happy colors. Pa loves to sing—"Ei du Scheenie, ei du Scheenie, ei du Scheenie Schnitzelbank!"

"Anna," Jed says. "What's a she-devil?"

"I don't know, Jed." She's probably a bad-tempered old Rebel who bakes Yankee children and their sweet fathers in her big black stove and then serves them to her kin for supper. But I don't tell my little brother that. I don't tell him a lot of things.

In my snug corner and hidden deep beneath the blue-and-white checked quilt Ma made for me before I was even born, I cry as rain pounds against the roof above.

"Anna." Jed parts the curtain that separates his side of the room from mine. "I can't sleep."

Sniffling back my tears, I open up my quilt for him to snuggle in beside me—all bony elbows and knees. But Jed doesn't snuggle in the way I'd like him to. He stands in front of me, skinny in his long johns, and says, "I have an idea. Remember 'Thumbelina'?"

"Of course." I love this story about a tiny girl who goes on a perilous journey. She meets such interesting characters and ends up marrying a flower prince with an aquiline nose! But I don't want to think about "Thumbelina" now.

"Remember the dead swallow part?" Jed's freckled face looks so serious. Oh I love my little brother—actually serious about "Thumbelina." He says, "Remember how Thumbelina finds a dead swallow stuck in the mud?"

"She finds it in an underground tunnel, Jed. And the swallow's not really dead. Thumbelina only thinks so because it lies so still." I must set the story straight. I am the family storyteller—Pa says. Tears flood my eyes.

"So what does she do for the swallow?" Jed says in a rutchety way. He hates it when I cry.

"She wraps him in a soft warm blanket." I have no idea where this is heading. Pa's been mortally infected two states away and we are telling tales.

"The next part is what got me thinking." Jed starts to pace the way Cousin Ezekiel does when a Holy Vision is about to come upon him. "Thumbelina rests her head on the swallow's breast and what does she hear? The swallow's heartbeat.

"Don't you see?" The way Jed almost shouts these words makes me sit bolt upright, tears and all. "Pa needs *us* to do the same! He needs to feel *us* lay our heads against *his* chest. He needs to hear us say—*Your heart's still beating, Pa. Wake up!*

"Anna . . . Why don't we just go to Winchester and save our pa?"

"Why don't we?" I say. *Because it's been nineteen days since that letter was written that said Pa was dying. He's probably already* . . . No. No! He's just in a deathlike trance! He just needs us to tell him that his heart's still beating. Jed's right.

"Well, why don't we!" I should have thought of this first. "Thumbelina" is *my* story. "I'll brew Pa boneset tea!" That miracle tea cured Cousin Ezekiel of a high fever that came on after I'd pulled his infected tooth. "I'll put healing Live-forever on Pa's wound!"

"You'll bake him apple dumplings and shoofly pie!"

"I'll rub Pa's head."

"You have healing hands, Anna."

"I have our ma's hands." My hands can feel out knotted muscles and knead them soft as bread. "But Jed, Winchester's so far away!"

"Only one hundred and eight miles. We could walk there!"

"Walk there? It'd take weeks."

"We'd walk fast."

"But we can't leave now. It's nighttime! It's raining! And we don't know how to get there!"

"We'll leave early in the morning and yes we do!" Jed disappears into his side of the room and a moment later he's back, waving a paper in my face. "This map shows the way! Before Pa left, he drew it for me."

"Pa should have drawn that map for me." I try to grab it from Jed.

Holding it out of reach, he says, "Boys are the ones who follow in their pas' footsteps."

"Not anymore!" Jed and I tussle over the map. As my fingers pry Jed's off the precious map, I hear footsteps followed by the click click click of dog nails. Cousin Ezekiel and Anarchy are going to bed. Jed and I stare at each other.

"We can't take Cousin Ezekiel to Winchester," Jed says.

"Someone has to stay behind to mind the farm." A sickening ache fills the pit of my stomach. I hate to leave Cousin Ezekiel. Who will darn the socks he's forever tearing? Who will make him corn pudding? What if he has a

Holy Vision with Samson and wanders off? Who will search for him? Will Miss Bemis? Will she bring him inside out of the rain?

Jed lights the lantern next to my bed and I flatten out Pa's map across my quilt. Seeing his familiar handwriting gives me a jolt. He's neatly printed place names, numbers, lines, dots, X's and two squares, one marked Winchester, the other, *Home*. Oh and look what he's done! He's drawn a little cave with bats hanging from the ceiling. Beside it is the printed word—*Cavetown*.

I know I have to go.

"Here's the path." Jed points to a dotted line that winds over what looks like squiggles of mountains, past Cavetown and across the broad line of a river. Seems to me I could follow that dotted line just as well as Jed. Seems to me that men and boys aren't the only ones who can go off to see the elephant.

THREE

At dawn, I guide a sleepy Cousin Ezekiel downstairs to the kitchen. I sit him at our blue table and he starts eating the last meal he'll share with us for a long time. "It'll be a good day to plant fence posts," he says while nibbling on a biscuit I baked for him in the middle of the night. "The ground will be soft and full of the glory of the Lord." He glances out the window. "Samson thinks so, too."

Out back in the muddy barnyard, Cousin Ezekiel's old plow horse sits on his big dappled gray hindquarters. He is contemplating the sun that rises over the nearby manure pile. I imagine Samson would think it's a good day for a journey to Winchester, too. I just wish Jed and I didn't have to walk the whole way there. But I'd never ask to borrow Samson. Cousin Ezekiel loves his horse too much to be parted from him. Besides, Samson is . . . a little odd.

Beside me, Jed sighs and starts jiggling his leg. He's ready to leave. Jed had wanted to sneak away without even telling Cousin Ezekiel goodbye. Jed had said, "It'll take too long!" I'd said, "No it won't! Let me do the talking! I know how to explain things to Cousin Ezekiel in gentle ways he understands."

"Cousin Ezekiel," I now say. "You remember 'Thumbelina.' "

"She popped out of a tulip," he says. I notice him noticing the packed bags Jed has propped beside the door. "Your pa loved tulips," Cousin Ezekiel says.

"Why are those bags packed?" he says.

"Jed and I are going on a journey." I take a deep breath and just as I'm about to explain it all by gently reminding Cousin Ezekiel of what little Thumbelina did, rutchety Jed jumps in and he tells it all himself! He talks so fast I can't even get a word in edgewise! He says: "Pa needs us now, Cousin Ezekiel! We have to go to him now! We know how—we have a map—we will save our pa the way Thumbelina saved the swallow, dying in the mud."

"We have swallows here," Cousin Ezekiel says in a tone that tells me he thinks he's taken in what Jed has said but doesn't want to address it yet. Cousin Ezekiel gets up from the table and peers out the window. "Look. There's the nest. Under the eaves."

In a protected spot, just beneath where the roof juts out, an empty nest is plastered to the side of our house. Beyond it, Samson still sits on his hindquarters, only now he's contemplating the kitchen.

"The swallows are gone right now," Cousin Ezekiel says.

"But they'll be back," I remind him.

"Last fall I left our house and I came back," he says. "Your pa took me to Baltimore to buy a pig!" They'd brought back our first and only pig, Lauden Honor. "On the way back home, we met a sutler. He sold me 'The Battle Hymn of the Republic.' Sutlers follow the armies. Did you know? Sutlers sell soldiers things they need like sheet music and mustache cream. But you must be wary of sutlers."

"We'll watch out for them." I pat Cousin Ezekiel's hand. "We'll be fine. And while we're gone, you'll be fine, too. I've made you biscuits—enough for a week. There's cheese and butter in the springhouse. Miss Bemis will bring you oatcakes.

"Before you know it, we'll be back with Pa!"

"I miss your pa." Cousin Ezekiel rubs his head. "But I don't see how you can save him, Anna. Nice girls don't travel through the Outside World where there are sutlers and soldiers and guns and someone might harm them."

"Thumbelina did," I say.

"She lived in Thumbelina country. You live in America and . . . America is at war." A clouded look comes over Cousin Ezekiel's eyes. If that look settles, he'll turn stubborn on me. He'll protest my going until kingdom come!

"Cousin Ezekiel, if I don't go to Winchester to save Pa, we won't have a home." It hurts for me to say this, but it's true.

"Anna shouldn't leave home," Cousin Ezekiel tells Jed. My little brother kicks the table leg. He's really angry. But I couldn't leave Cousin Ezekiel without talking to him! He says, "Truth is, girls stay at home."

I think for a minute. "What if I'm not a girl?" I say. "What if . . . what if I'm a boy? What if I go to Winchester disguised as a boy?" I can't believe that I just said this. Imagine, wearing trousers! No girl I know has ever worn trousers.

"We'd have to cut off your hair," Jed says. He knows how I feel about my hair! My long dark hair is the prettiest thing about me.

"I'll tie my hair back," I say.

"If we don't cut your hair, you're still a girl." Jed's got his skinny shoulders squared and a determined look on his face.

"Would you let me leave home if I let you cut off my hair?" I ask Cousin Ezekiel. *My beautiful dark curls.*

He nods. He doesn't think I'll do it.

"Then cut it," I say.

"But I . . . I'll miss you, Anna." Tears fill Cousin Ezekiel's eyes. He looks away. He stares out the window. Samson's still out there sitting on his hindquarters and staring at the house.

Jed kicks at the table leg. Again. I get up from the table, go over and put my arms around Cousin Ezekiel. I rest my cheek against his back. "We have to go, Cousin Ezekiel. You know that."

"I know." He continues staring out the window. When at last he turns to me, his eyes are still filled with tears—only now, they're bright and shining. "You can go. You and Jed can leave me. But only if you go as a boy. And only if . . . if Samson goes with you! Samson has to go with you. Samson will keep you safe. Samson will bring you and your pa back to me."

"No! Not Samson! *You* need him." *We can't take Samson.*

"Samson doesn't belong in Rebel country," Jed says.

"Don't you see, Cousin Ezekiel?" I try to be as gentle as I can. "Samson only obeys Bible commands and he's so hard of hearing. To get him to move forward, we'd have to shout—'Love thy neighbor, Samson!' All those dirty Rebels would think we were talking about them."

"I taught that horse well." Cousin Ezekiel smiles through his tears. I feel as if my heart will break. *He's willing to give us Samson.* "You can depend on Samson," Cousin Ezekiel says. "And I . . . I can, too."

FOUR DARK CURLS COVER OUR

kitchen floor. My curls. Used to be I could pin them up. Loose, they'd bob against my back. Cousin Ezekiel's scissors snip away while our dog, Anarchy, looks at me with one ear cocked. When Cousin Ezekiel finally says, "I'm done," I reach up to touch what little hair I have left. Jed studies me. Jed says, "You don't look like Anna now."

"I need a boy's name." My throat aches. All my long soft curls are gone. "I want it to start with A like Anna."

"A could be for Adam," Jed says.

"Adam then. Call me Adam. Adam was brave. He started the human race." Thinking of what Adam did and what I'm about to do, I almost burst into tears. But I don't want Cousin Ezekiel to see me cry and so I don't.

He gives us a leg up on his Samson, eighteen hands high and weighing, I am sure, two tons. In the bags behind Jed are packed what we now need for our journey, including: oatcakes for Samson, biscuits and a change of underclothes for us, Pa's paint box (Pa loves to paint), *The 1863 Farmer's Almanac*, a piece of clay to remind Pa of home and now Cousin Ezekiel's pocket Bible, which he's just handed me because, as he says, "You can't go traveling through war without one."

"Now what am I supposed to tell Miss Bemis when she finds out you're gone?" he says.

"You're to tell her we've gone to visit our . . . Aunt Winnie," I say as Samson swings his bridled head around to nuzzle me. Ugly me. Pa's battered gray felt hat now covers my chopped-off hair, I wear a gray wool jacket and itchy trousers that once belonged to Sybil Freeman's oldest brother, Robert, and my feet swim in a pair of Cousin Ezekiel's old brogans. Will I pass as a boy now? I'd better!

"You don't have an Aunt Winnie," Cousin Ezekiel says.

"Aunt Winnie is our code name for Winchester!" Jed says. We've already told this to Cousin Ezekiel three times.

"What does Aunt Winnie look like?" he says.

"Tall with stringy hair and several missing teeth." I answer the way I think Adam would. Now that I'm disguised as Adam, I'd better learn to talk like him. It'd be too dangerous not to—me, not only a girl in disguise, but a Yankee girl at that and traveling into Rebel country.

"A sutler could sell Aunt Winnie new teeth," Cousin Ezekiel says. "Mine sold me Samson's favorite hymn— 'The Battle Hymn of the Republic.'

"Now you be sure to feed Samson two of Miss Bemis's oatcakes every day. They're good for his bowels." Cousin Ezekiel hugs Samson's head. The old horse blows out his nose and sighs. I hate to part the two of them—*but it's getting late.* Across the street, Miss Bemis's pet pig, Charity, squeals her hunger cry. Miss Bemis, with a swill pail of pig food, is waddling down her front steps. If she comes closer, she'll see through my disguise! She'll stop me from saving Pa! "Cousin Ezekiel!"

He gives Samson a final pat and then steps aside.

I give Samson the command to move forward—"Love thy neighbor, Samson!"

Samson doesn't move.

"You have to say it louder than that," Cousin Ezekiel says.

I clear my throat. "Love thy neighbor, Samson!"

Samson twitches his ears, but he still doesn't move.

From across the street, Miss Bemis looks our way. "Anna? Jed?" she calls out.

I pull down my hat to hide my head. "Love thy neighbor, Samson!" I shout and Jed shouts, too. We drum our heels against Samson's sides. He sighs and then breaks into an easy jog. He slowly carries us away. Are we on our way? We are! We've escaped Miss Bemis! Now if only we can get past all the other people in New Oxford who know me.

We pass a small fishing pond near our farm. Beyond it lies Pastor Hogenboom's stretch of land marked by its long line of poplar trees. I hope the pastor's not out wandering. He'll stop us for certain.

"We must get quickly to Winchester, save Pa and bring him quickly back," I tell Jed.

"I have Pa's map. First we travel the pike to Gettysburg," Jed says. That's easy. Gettysburg is only eight miles from here. Every fall we travel to Gettysburg to buy shoes.

"On the other side of Gettysburg lies South Mountain," Jed continues. "We'll spend our first night at the foot of it. The next day, we hike up the mountain."

"I hope it's not steep." I like things flat and I'm sure Samson does, too. Jed and I are already settling into his jog. I like riding in trousers instead of a skirt. It's easier.

"It should take less than two days to reach our next main stop—Cavetown," Jed says. I remember those little bats Pa drew to mark the place. "From there, we travel eighteen miles to Williamsport where we ford the Potomac River into Virginia. You know the Potomac's the dividing line between the North and South," the great collector of facts says.

"I know that, Jed."

"General Robert E. Lee crossed the dividing line once. Lee tried to invade the North. But we stopped him at Antietam. . . . Did you know the Rebels on the south side of the Potomac have horns like the devil? They boil babies alive!"

"I've heard that, Jed." I don't even have time to worry about these babies, however, because I must deal with a more immediate concern. Pastor Hogenboom. Suddenly, black coattails flying, he hurries down the brick path leading out from his small gray clapboard house that's just ahead.

"What do we do now?" I hiss back at my little brother.

"Just tip your hat and keep Samson moving."

I pull Pa's cap down to the middle of my forehead and leave it there. As we near Pastor Hogenboom, he squints at us through the spectacles perched on his small up-turned nose. He calls out from his front gate, "Now, is that you, Jed Sunday?"

The pastor doesn't acknowledge me. Good.

"Good day, Pastor Hogenboom!" Jed says far too brightly, because Samson, who's always eager to nuzzle anyone we happen to *brightly* greet, comes to an abrupt halt. I curl my hands into Samson's fluffy mane and stare down as the pastor approaches. His plump hand runs down Samson's neck and he says, "It's a sunny Saturday, ain't it? Where might you be going?"

"Off to visit my Aunt Winnie," Jed says. "This here's my cousin and her son. Adam can't hear and he's mute besides.

"Adam's feeling rutchety right now," Jed rattles on. "He lives near Gettysburg and I told him I'd get him there as soon as I can. His brother Stanley, who's been off at war, is visiting Gettysburg for the day; we don't want to miss him."

"Well of course you don't." Pastor Hogenboom touches my arm. "You look familiar, Adam."

I don't look up.

"Adam sometimes comes to church with me," Jed says. The pastor continues to keep his hand on my arm. I can't breathe. After several *long* moments, he pats my arm and says, "Well, you go on now and a happy journey to you."

Since I am mute, I leave it up to Jed to give Samson his

command to move forward. This time the old horse moves right out. It's only when we are well beyond the pastor's sight that I say, "I don't want to see anyone else I know. Not one person, Jed. Not even one!"

"I feel badly—fibbing to Pastor Hogenboom." Jed ignores what I've just said. "But I didn't exactly fib, did I, Anna? We are off to see Aunt Winnie, right?"

"Who's this cousin Stanley we're supposed to see?" I whisper back at Jed. Stanley must exist somewhere. Jed couldn't just invent him.

"Stanley Bemis! He wrote the letter about Pa!"

"Oh. That Stanley." He's a pompous goose. Whenever he visits, Miss Bemis has us over for dinner and the two of them correct Jed's and my table manners.

"When we get to Winchester, we'll need to find Stanley to find Pa," Jed says.

"Oh curses!" To that and to the right fork in the road ahead that I know we're supposed to take to reach the Gettysburg Pike. The right fork runs past the homes of two more people who know me too well—Hans Yoder and Sybil Freeman. The left fork, on the other hand, is an overgrown back road. There's no one along it who would recognize me. It leads to Gettysburg, too. I shout, "Samson! Lean on the Lord!" *Turn left!*

"No Anna!" Jed shouts in my ear. "To turn right, you shout—'Samson! Repent and be saved!' "

"Samson! Lean on the Lord!" I repeat. Samson obeys my command to turn left so easily, you'd think it was the back road he was meant to take anyway. Two scrawny old buzzards lift off the dead branch of an oak tree that we pass.

"This isn't on Pa's map!" Jed yells at me. "This is a mistake."

"No it's not," I say in the confident way I think a boy named Adam would. "Don't you see? There's no one along this back road who knows us. No one to stop us. We are free at last!

"Hang on, Pa! We're coming!"

PART TWO

The Journey

FIVE

IT'S BEEN FIVE HOURS
since we were at a fork in the road and I commanded
Samson to *lean on the Lord.* I'd give anything to be at
that fork again. This time I'd yell—*Repent and be saved!*
I'd forgotten that the back road had *three* forks in it. We're
lost and it's almost nightfall. We should have reached
Gettysburg three hours ago.

"So *Adam,* what do we do now?" Jed says. The dirt
road we've been following the past hour has petered out
into a rain-swollen stream. To our left, a deep forest covers a chilly-looking hilltop. To our right, the sun has
started to go down over a steep walled-in farmer's field—
plowed and muddy.

"We could retrace our steps," I say.

"We don't have time." Jed shivers in the damp wind.
I shiver, too. Samson, snorting, shakes his head and pulls
the reins out of my hands. With Jed and me on board, he
heads toward the farmer's field. "Are you going to let him
wander?" Jed asks.

"I don't think he's wandering." We watch Samson

nose open a little iron gate. Keeping the low stone wall on his left, Samson walks up a muddy furrow, then stops a moment to sniff the wind before walking on. "I think he's sniffing out a friendly someone to point us in the right direction! He always does this when he and Cousin Ezekiel get lost. Let's just let Samson go his own way and have faith," I say.

Pa has said that faith means going out not knowing, but trusting in the Lord. So Jed and I trust in the Lord to guide our Samson. Only something gets in the way. That something is a huge black dog that comes hurtling out of nowhere! With bared teeth, the dog throws himself at Samson! He nips at Samson's heels!

"Bad dog!" I scream. Jed yells, "YOUGETOUTA-HERE!" Samson bucks! Samson kicks at the dog! Samson scrambles in the mud and then, he tears off at a gallop with the black dog barking at his heels. That fierce black dog sends Samson galloping up the field, over the low stone wall and into the forest with Jed clinging to me, and me clinging to Samson and screaming at him to stop—"Amen, Brother Samson! Amen!"

With lowered head, our thirsty Bible horse takes long drafts of pond water. He'd run and run—there'd been no stopping him until he was deep into the woods. He brought us here to this lonely pond that seems as deep and quiet as the woods surrounding it. I have no idea where we are now. We could be halfway to Cavetown, Maryland, with the little bats Pa drew or clear the way north in New York State.

The sun's gone down. I'm cold. My legs ache from

riding Samson. My stomach aches. So does my heart. *We're so lost.* Behind me, Jed's fallen asleep with his cheek pressed against my back.

Samson lifts his head, backs out of the pond and moves out. He follows a muddy cattle path through the wet-leaf-smelling woods in the direction of a new moon rising in the sky. Maybe Samson still knows where he's going.

"Where are we?" Jed says in a sleepy voice.

"Still in the woods. But Samson's on his way to some-where." My voice breaks. Jed, not seeming to notice, says, "My bucket's full."

"Amen, Brother Samson!" I shout. Samson halts and Jed slides off to relieve himself. Moments later, he's back. He looks up at me and says, "Now how do I get back on?"

"I don't know." Cousin Ezekiel has always been around to help us mount Samson.

"Give me a hand," Jed says.

Jed backs off a little to get a running start. As I pull, he flings himself up on Samson. Jed gets his right leg onto a pack.

"You can do it, Jed!" I say and, halfway on, he starts to giggle. Seeing Jed's scrawny leg trying to inch itself over our huge packs makes me giggle, too. Our giggles turn to laughter. Still holding on to my hand, Jed slides toward the ground. I'm now laughing so hard, I can't stop him. A moment later, it's not only Jed on the muddy ground, but also me. We look at each other and laugh so hard we cry.

Walking with Samson between us, we follow the muddy cattle path Samson had discovered earlier. It winds on and on through an ever-darkening forest, curving through damp brush to a muddy stream and then mounting to a low ridge. Suddenly, it takes a turn up a steep hill. Climbing steep hills makes me tired. I look for a sign to tell me this hill is worth climbing. That's when I see the wagon ruts in the path ahead.

I point them out to Jed. "They look fresh! This must be a road, Jed. A road must have joined the cattle path somewhere in the woods and we didn't even realize it— although I'm sure Samson did! Do you know where I think this road leads?"

"To your friendly someone who can help us mount our horse and point the way to Gettysburg!" he says.

"Better than that! I think it leads to a warm brick house. It will have good kind people living in it. We'll tell them we got lost trying to find our Aunt Winnie who lives near Gettysburg. 'Oh you poor children,' they'll say. 'We'll show you the way to Gettysburg, but first, do come and share our supper with us. And would you like to spend the night?'

"Let's go find these people, Jed." The steep hill we climb turns rocky. My feet start to hurt. Cousin Ezekiel's brogans are too big! Wish I could go barefoot. Even young ladies can go barefoot, once the bloom is on the dogwood trees—Pa's rule. An owl hoots from somewhere in the towering trees ahead. Another owl hoots back. Something rustles in the brush off to our left.

"What's that?" Jed says.

"It's just a squirrel." I hope it's a squirrel. It could be a wolf. *Or a Rebel.* But in Pennsylvania? Even when Lee crossed the Potomac last fall, he only got as far as Maryland.

"I smell something," Jed says.

I sniff the air. I smell it, too. "It's wood smoke, Jed. And . . . roasting pork! Maybe the good kind people will be serving sauerkraut, mashed potatoes and apple dumplings to go along with it."

We pick up our pace. Samson breaks into a jog. The three of us hurry toward what I hope will be a sweet brick house with smoke pouring out of its chimney. I grow so lightheaded with this hope, the steep climb and the smell of roasting meat that I'm totally unprepared for what comes next—

A voice out of nowhere shouting, "Stop right where you are!"

Startled, Samson stops so fast, he sits backward onto his hindquarters and I fall onto mine.

"You dirty devils," a man's voice says. The cold bore of a rifle brushes against my cheek. Now it pokes against my chattering teeth. "I should tear your arms out by the roots and beat you with the bloody ends of them. Thinking you could sneak up here to ambush my good friend Roscoe and me."

SIX

THE MAN WHO HAS threatened to tear out our arms and beat us with the bloody ends of them is not quite as scary looking as he sounds. He's so thin he must weigh less than I do. He's dressed like a gentleman in a fancy vest with silver dragons on it. Unlike Pa and Cousin Ezekiel, he has no fine thick beard, only a wispy black mustache that he's waxed to make the ends curl up.

He prods Jed and me to our feet with his rifle butt. "If you two don't behave yourselves, I'll not only tear out your arms, but also have you both beheaded because I'm the descendant of a Welsh king—Griffydd, King of Wales—and that's what Welsh kings do!" he says in a peculiar accent I have never before heard. He goes on to call us—"Spies for the Hounds of Hell."

"We're no spies." My voice sounds weak and trembly—not like the brave Adam I'm supposed to be. I hope this Welshman doesn't sense my disguise! I clear my throat and force myself to say, "We just got lost, that's all."

The Welshman hands Samson's reins over to what must be the Welshman's *good friend Roscoe.* He's a colored boy with black skin, dark brown eyes and bushy hair. He looks to be my age, maybe a little older. Is he a slave? If so, then this Welshman must be a slave owner and a dirty Rebel, too, because us Yankees don't own slaves and we never will!

The Welshman prods Jed and me off the path and over to the stone foundation of a house that I had hoped would be a home like mine. But this house is nothing but an unfinished rectangle of cold gray stone with a pig roasting over a fire in the middle of it. I was hungry for roast pork. But not now—my appetite has fled.

The Welshman gestures for Jed and me to sit down. Two large boulders become our chairs—Jed's arm pressed against mine. With a rope, the Welshman binds my hands together while my teeth chatter. As he binds Jed's hands, the Welshman says, "This all smells of One-Eyed Pete's wily schemes. He should have come himself, the surly coward."

Something in the way the Welshman talks reminds me of myself when I am telling stories and trying to act the part of someone else. Something tells me that this Welshman, who must be only in his early twenties, is not as fierce as he makes himself out to be. I just don't know. He ties my left leg to Jed's right while Roscoe leads Samson past us. Seeing Roscoe's hand on Samson's reins makes me want to cry out—"You can't take Samson! How will we get to Pa?" But I keep my silence. I don't want Roscoe or the Welshman to know anything about Jed and me.

"Look at that fine-looking horse! What strong legs!

What a fine broad chest and back," the Welshman says as Roscoe tethers Samson next to a swaybacked chestnut mare grazing at the clearing's edge. She raises her head, pins back her ears and bares her teeth at our fine horse. He sidles backward into a covered wagon with a fierce red dragon painted on its canvas. It's got a two-horse hitch, but only one horse. Where's the other one?

The Welshman crouches in front of me so that his hazel eyes are level with mine. He says, "If you're not minions for One-Eyed Pete, why are you here?" I keep silent. I don't know what minions are and I'm afraid to ask.

The Welshman grins. Young as he is, he has three gold teeth up top and two dark holes where teeth should be on the bottom.

"We're here because my bucket was full," Jed pipes up. He has an earnest expression on his face that I know well. Jed is going to be brave and save us both by telling the truth—at least the truth as he sees it.

"Jed got off Samson—that's our horse—to relieve himself." I press a warning arm against Jed—*watch what you say*. "Samson's so big, Jed couldn't get back on."

"Anna here tried to help me. We both got the giggles."
Anna? Did Jed just call me Anna?

The man's grin grows wider. He's so close I can smell his breath. It smells heavy-sweet, like the Dr. Erastus Cure-all Cousin Ezekiel takes to ease the suffering brought on when he has a toothache.

"Anna laughed so hard, she fell off Samson." Jed looks triumphantly at me. The Welshman, a merry look in his eyes, looks at me, too. I feel myself go numb all over.

"There we were, the two of us, laughing on the ground; we laughed so hard we cried," Jed says. "All we need now is for you to give us a leg up on Samson and point us in the right direction. Then, we'll be on our way."

"And where would that way be?" The Welshman is still eyeing me.

"To visit our Aunt Winnie," I say. I don't want Jed talking about our Yankee pa. We mustn't trust this slick-talking Welshman. He could be a Rebel spy! "She's tall and sickly." I stop myself from saying that she has missing teeth.

The Welshman sits back on his heels and says, "I have a riddle for you both:

> Dean Swift often speaks of a
> Queen whose name
> Read backward or forward is
> Always the same.

"Who would that queen be?" he says.

"That's easy!" Jed, the eager collector of facts, says. "Our pa read us that from The *Farmer's Almanac*. The answer is Anna."

With a long and elegant looking finger, the *Rebel* flicks off my cap, revealing my chopped-off hair. The blood drains from my face. "Would you call this Anna a queen?" he says.

"I would. My pa does." Suddenly, Jed's face turns as white as mine must be. He realizes his mistake. But fear makes his tongue wag even harder. "My pa calls our Anna—Queen of Apple Dumplings."

Roscoe, coming up behind the *Rebel*, says, "This here's a queen?" Roscoe stares at me in obvious disbelief. "If you's a queen, how come you dress so raggedy, like some farmer boy?"

Jed jumps in and answers for me. "Anna's dressed as a boy, because if she didn't, you Rebels might see how pretty she is and take advantage of her." So Jed thinks they're Rebels, too!

"Us Rebels?" Roscoe laughs. "Whhoooo-eee. You is some kind of funny."

"He is not." I need to stand up for myself and Jed as well. "You Rebels hurt everything you can get your hands on. Why you . . . why you boil babies alive!"

"Mister Eli," Roscoe says. "This here queen thinks we're baby-boiling Rebels!"

The Rebel named Mister Eli laughs.

"Mister Eli is no Rebel and I'm no Rebel, neither," Roscoe says. "No free colored man is. Leastways, not the kind you mean. My daddy's joined the Union Army! He's a private in the Fifty-fourth Massachusetts Infantry and he means to fight to set all our people free."

"Our pa's a private, too," Jed says. "He serves with the Eighty-seventh Regiment of Pennsylvania Volunteers."

"Where's your ma?" Mister Eli says softly.

"She's dead," Jed says. "But our pa isn't. Our pa's first name is Abraham. As in Abraham Lincoln, the President of these United States of America. So you'd better treat us kindly."

"Whooo-eee!" Roscoe says.

"Roscoe, my friend," Mister Eli says, "these two are no minions of One-Eyed Pete. What we have here are

Anna, Queen of Apple Dumplings, and President Lincoln's son! And they have a magnificent horse!" As quickly as he bound our hands together, Mister Eli frees them. He unbinds our legs and our feet, too.

"Can we go now?" I'm a little surprised by the swift turn of events, but I'll accept them. Maybe Mister Eli and Roscoe are friendly someones, even though they look and act a little strange. Maybe they think that Jed and I are friendly someones, too.

"Don't go now," Mister Eli says with a new warmth in his voice. "You must be tired and hungry. So must your horse." He turns to Roscoe. "My good friend. Offer that magnificent horse two quarts of Miss Dixie's bran meal. Then set two more places at our dining table while I break out the canned oysters, ginger pop and Mrs. Staple's sweet cake. Tonight, we're entertaining royalty."

SEVEN

MISTER ELI, THE Welshman who is *not* a Rebel, presents Jed and me with interesting news. We are already south of Gettysburg and only a fifteen-minute walk from South Mountain. I knew Samson had us headed in the right direction! "I trust you're not going to try and cross that mountain on your own," Mister Eli says. "It's a dangerous place—full of Rebel spies. And bloody-minded miscreants like One-Eyed Pete."

"Aunt Winnie lives on this side of the mountain. At the foot," I say as Jed and I exchange an anxious glance. In truth, we must cross that dangerous mountain to get to Pa.

"Tomorrow, early, we'll head you in the right direction," Mister Eli says. "Meanwhile, let us forget about the baser elements of society who lurk in mountain woods and caves. Let us rejoice with one another and have a grand feast!"

I soon learn that almost everything about Mister Eli is

grand. For one thing, he's rich! His wagon's full of treasures—from men's trousers, to ladies' bonnets, to canned oysters and a newfangled drink he insists Jed and I try at supper—ginger pop. For another, his family back in southern Wales owns thousands of acres of land in a green and misty spot Mister Eli calls the "Vale of Glamorgan." Carpets of yellow flowers, dotted with white clouds of grazing sheep, cover the fields in front of his family's huge stone castle.

I hug myself. Even the word *castle* sounds magical. Mister Eli says that behind his *castle* rises a steep, rocky and *enchanted* slope!

"Underground tunnels run all through this slope," he says, eating a canned oyster from what he calls his throne—a red and green striped canvas chair. "The tunnels lead to a grand cave with ceilings thirty feet high! The fairy folk gather there on rainy nights to sip mead and dance the minuet.

"A mammoth boulder shaped like a chair stands guard at the entrance to the fairies' cave," he continues. "They say if a mortal spends the night in that chair, he becomes a poet or a madman."

"You slept on that stone chair, now didn't you, Mister Eli," Roscoe says.

Mister Eli laughs. "I did, indeed. Two days later, I walked out of our stone castle and boarded a boat bound for America. What does that make me, Roscoe?"

"A poet!" Roscoe grins. He has on a black bow tie that Mister Eli gave him to wear in honor of the royal guests— Jed and me. Jed has on a black tie, too. Mister Eli says these ties make the two of them look quite "debonair." He offered me a green velvet bonnet with white roses and lace to wear. He said it came all the way from the Court of the Empress Eugénie in Paris, France. I declined the bonnet. I didn't want to be beholden to a man I'm still unsure of.

"Here's to poets everywhere!" Mister Eli raises a tin cup filled with ginger pop. Jed, Roscoe and I raise ours. We three drink to poets, and the ginger pop Mister Eli poured for me fizzles in my mouth. I like the drink. However, it has a bitter aftertaste that reminds me of some medicine I once took. I swallow it quickly.

Mister Eli spears another oyster. To please him, I decide to try the oyster he gave me along with roast pork and canned asparagus. When I spear the oyster, it wobbles.

"Ever eaten a live oyster, Anna, Queen of Apple Dumplings?" Mister Eli asks as I stare at the insides of the canned oyster I've forked open—a mushy green and gray. I shake my head no. My head is starting to feel fuzzy. It must be the damp night air.

"I ate my first oyster three years ago," Mister Eli says. I push mine beneath one of the biscuits Jed and I contributed to the royal feast. "The Duke of Argyle and I were in Baltimore and we came upon one of its fine oyster houses. We swallowed one live oyster after another—right from the shell. I said to myself, 'Ah, this is heaven indeed. If only all of life could be as easy as an oyster going down.' "

"Our pa's been to Baltimore," Jed says. "He went there with our Cousin Ezekiel to buy a pig."

"Cousin Ezekiel?" Mister Eli looks around the campfire as if he fears our cousin might pop out of the surrounding darkness and attack him. Mister Eli is certainly on edge. But no wonder. South Mountain with its bloodcurdling miscreants is only a fifteen-minute walk away!

"Cousin Ezekiel's back at our farm," I say quickly. "He loves our farm. He's only ever left it once and that was to go with Pa to Baltimore.

"They brought back a very special pig," I add. "His name is Lauden Honor."

"My family kept pigs," Mister Eli says, which surprises me. I didn't know fancy people in castles kept pigs. He says, "I remember being seven years of age and we had seven piglets. I named them after King Arthur and his knights.

"What a mistake." Tears brim in Mister Eli's eyes. His voice goes soft. "You must never name any creature you mean to eat. When Lancelot met his fate with Tommy Jones, the butcher, I wept. And then, there was little Gawain who became the pork roast for Easter dinner."

"Oh, but we'd never eat Lauden Honor," I say.

"We bred him to Miss Bemis's pet pig, Charity," Jed says. "Soon, they'll be having piglets."

"They will?" I've never heard anything about this.

"Cousin Ezekiel whispered to me that there just might be some piglets when we get home, and won't the Lord be pleased!" Jed says.

"Here's to Cousin Ezekiel, who has the good sense to stay at home and breed pigs!" Mister Eli raises his cup in another toast. "Drink up, everyone! Drink up!"

"To Cousin Ezekiel." I drain my cup, and as I do, I get a strange tingling in my throat. It bubbles all the way down my chest and into my stomach.

Mister Eli pours us all more ginger pop. "Drink up, Anna, Queen of Apple Dumplings," he says.

"No." The word feels funny in my mouth. I say it again, "No. I'm not a queen. I'm a boy now." Boys get to follow in their father's footsteps. Boys get to hear about breeding pigs! "I am Adam. You must all call me Adam!"

"All right, *Adam*," Mister Eli says.

I down my second cup of the funny-tasting ginger pop and that's when I start to notice the dragons. A dragon seems to be spitting fire from the metal pitcher Mister Eli uses to pour our drinks. I count seventeen silver dragons on Mister Eli's vest. And then there's that huge red dragon on Mister Eli's wagon. I get to my feet and stumble over to pet this dragon, for I like the expression of defiance in its eyes.

Samson nickers "hello" to me and so I visit with him first. I throw my arms around his neck. He reaches around my back and dips his nose into my empty pocket in hopes of finding oatcakes. It feels as if Samson's hugging me. He's warm. He's my blanket. My big, nuzzly, dappled gray blanket.

"I've admired your horse ever since you arrived," Mister Eli says.

"What happened to your second horse?" I point to the two-horse hitch I'd noticed earlier. My finger feels as fuzzy as my head.

"He died, unfortunately," Mister Eli says.

"Oh." I try to smile how sorry I am for Mister Eli, but my mouth's too numb.

"It's been hard on Dixie—pulling a heavy wagon by herself." Mister Eli pets the swaybacked mare who's got her nasty ears pinned back. "She's got a long trip ahead."

"Where's she going?" I ask.

"Oh someplace far away . . . Your fine upstanding Yankee horse would make a fine team mate for her," he says.

"Samson's not for sale." Things don't feel quite right here. Perhaps Jed and I should leave. Only there's the dark. And that mountain. And my fuzzy head. "I feel a little strange."

"You've had a long day and now it's evening. You need to rest." Mister Eli smiles. He guides me over to my little brother. I can hardly walk.

Wrapped in a blanket, Jed lies on the ground with his head resting on one of our packs.

"When did Jed go to sleep?" I ask.

"Hours ago," Mister Eli says.

"It feels like seconds. Time passes quickly here. Must be the ginger pop. It tasted of—" I want to say medicine. Instead I say, "dragon's breath."

"Now you just go to sleep. Tomorrow you'll awaken as chipper as a dandy." Mister Eli helps me to lie down on a blanket that's been spread out next to Jed. I sprawl onto my back. Oh. Here's Roscoe. His tie is crooked.

"Will they be all right?" I hear him ask Mister Eli.

"They'll be fine." Mister Eli arranges a pack beneath my head and turns me so that I face Jed. Spit bubbles out one corner of my little brother's mouth. I want to wipe the spit away, but it's too much of an effort.

Mister Eli tucks the blanket around me, then he sits down on a rock and sings a lullaby to Jed and me:

Sleep my child and peace attend thee,
All through the night.
Guardian angels God will send thee
All through the night. . . .

"My Mo-ma says you have the voice of an angel, Mister Eli," Roscoe says when the singing's done. I'd agree, but now my mouth's so numb, I can't speak at all.

"Well, Roscoe, a sutler must have something going for him," Mister Eli says.

A *sutler?* I've heard that word, I think as I spin off into darkness. Cousin Ezekiel bought something off a sutler. I think it was a song. Or was it a dragon? He said it cost him fifteen cents.

EIGHT

ALL THROUGH THE night, I dream a guardian angel holds me in her arms. She smells of wet leaves and canvas and her skin is rough, but warm. She sings to me in a low-pitched voice that breaks each time she hits a high note. I try not to giggle. But the harder I try, the bigger my giggle grows. Finally, it grows so big, I just can't hold it anymore.

The angel hugs me as I laugh. She kisses the top of my head. In a voice that's deepened now, that doesn't sound like the angel's voice but like my pa's, she says, "Hush now, Anna. Sleep my apple dumpling queen."

Is that you, Pa? I've missed you! Cousin Ezekiel bred Lauden Honor to Charity and no one even told me.

"Wake up!" The angel who I dream is Pa shakes me.

I can't wake up; I can't open my eyes. I sink back into sleep; sweet sleep. Now the angel's shaking me again. But it can't be an angel; angels let sleepy girls sleep. I force my eyelids open. I see two dark eyes staring at me from out of an even darker face. This is no angel. This is Roscoe.

"You've got to help me," he whispers. "I've got your

horse all nicely harnessed next to Dixie. I goes to make him move out and he lays down on me."

"My horse? Samson? Where are you taking Samson?" I struggle to get the words out; my mouth is full of sleepy cobwebs.

"Ah . . . Nowhere special." Roscoe's still whispering and even in my sleepy cobwebbed state I can tell he's lying. "But if Mister Eli wakes up and finds I got a sleeping-down horse and a wagon that hasn't moved, he'll be so angry, every little creek this side of the Mississippi is gonna feel it and run backwards."

"It's good for creeks to run backwards." I close my heavy, sleepy eyes. I see stars on the backside of my eyelids now. In my mind, I draw a golden line connecting one star to the next.

"Wake up, Anna!" It's Roscoe again. How much time's gone by? It's still night out, a chilly dark. Roscoe sits me up and Jed, who's been curled warm and toasty against my back, sprawls forward onto my blanket and hides his head beneath one arm.

"Drink this." Roscoe hands me a cup of steaming coffee. I breathe in the fumes, sip coffee and stare dumb-eyed at the burning coals of last night's fire. Gray smoke drifts upward in a single thread. I imagine the smoky thread connecting all the stars together. The smoke and stars all spell a word—

S-U-T-L-E-R.

"Mister Eli is a sutler!" I announce.

"Mister Eli's a purveyor of all that's fine in this here

world. And don't you say one nasty word against him. Why, just two days ago, he helped me find out where my daddy is!"

"He gave Jed and me something funny tasting. It . . . it put us to sleep." As I say this, I realize it's the truth and I feel sick. Why would anyone *do* such a horrible thing? "He put something in that ginger pop!"

"Ain't nothing he didn't take himself. Just a little laudanum to help with sleep. Mister Eli has trouble sleeping account of that rotten tooth he's got," Roscoe says. "Why, he had to take a double shot of laudanum last night. He's sleeping like a baby now—all cozy in his wagon."

"Samson's hitched to that wagon. That's why Mister Eli gave Jed and me laudanum! He wanted to steal Samson while we slept!" I struggle to my feet. Oh I'm thinking clearly now. I must unharness Samson, throw a sleeping Jed across Samson's back and we'll head out for Pa. Which way would that be?

Across the mountain.

"I ain't done nothing to hurt your horse," Roscoe says as I stumble over to Samson. "I fed him same as I fed Dixie. I talked to him real nice. But after I got him hitched beside her, he just up and lay down on me."

"And he'll stay laying down on you until kingdom come, because Samson is our horse, not yours." Samson gazes up at me with a bewildered look in his eyes. He's never been hitched beside another horse. Nor been asked to move forward without first hearing the word of the Lord. "They had no right to do this to you, Samson." I try to unbuckle the traces, but my hands feel clumsy. Probably from the laudanum that horrible Mister Eli gave me.

Roscoe steps in and he helps me unbuckle the traces. Why? Does he think that once I get Samson standing, he can hitch him back up to Mister Eli's wagon and be off to someplace far away? Well, he can't!

I unlatch the final buckle and then I shout at Samson, "Arise, my love, my fair one!" Samson looks up at me, and in his horsey way, he smiles. Samson loves this passage from the Holy Bible. I pull on Samson's reins and shout, "The winter is past!" A smiling Samson stretches out his neck. "The time of singing has come!" I shout as I pull a little harder. Samson gathers his feet beneath him. I pull the third time and shout the finale—"And the voice of the turtledove is heard in our land!"

"I know them words!" Roscoe says while Samson rises majestically to his feet and shakes himself from nose to tail. "Them words come from the Song of Solomon! My Mo-ma says them each and every morning she gets up."

"Well, good for her." Samson reaches over and nibbles at my shirt. I wrap my arms around his head. "Oh Samson, they tried to steal you."

"We was just borrowing. We'd return him sooner or later," Roscoe says. "Besides, you're just visiting your Aunt Winnie. Mister Eli and me, we got to be clear across the wide mountain and to Cavetown by the day after tomorrow! And yesterday, our lead horse, old Cadwallader, up and died!"

"You're crossing the wide mountain full of Rebel spies and miscreants?" I say.

"Mister Eli's got himself a gun."

"And you're going to Cavetown?" Samson nudges me as I say the name. "Why Cavetown?"

"To buy . . ." Roscoe seems to be searching for something he has to buy. He comes upon it with a big wide grin. He pets Samson's nose and says, "To buy shoes. From Owen Glendower. He's Mister Eli's Cavetown friend. Mister Eli's got a regiment of soldiers waiting in Winchester, Virginia, for them . . . shoes."

"You and Mister Eli are going to Winchester?"

"We surely are."

Well what do I do now? Do I work out an arrangement with Roscoe? Can I trust him? He's allied with that horrible Mister Eli! But there's the mountain . . . I gaze into Samson's thoughtful eyes. He's the one who brought us here. He reaches out and nuzzles Roscoe's stomach.

"Roscoe," I say softly, "do you believe in God?"

NINE

believes in God, he also believes that if you have faith in God and are willing to go out not knowing, God can team you up with unlikely people who can help you reach your destination, which in Jed's and my case, happens to be Winchester. Yes, Jed and I are going to Winchester, too. Aunt Winnie is our code name for the Rebel town. As I am telling Roscoe this, Samson rests his mouth on Roscoe's shoulder, which reassures me that I have made the right choice. I can trust this boy.

I explain everything to Roscoe, from the time Miss Bemis read that letter about Pa to the moment Mister Eli leapt out of the darkness at Jed and me. And even though it's dark and I can't see Roscoe clearly, I can sense he's kind and understanding by the way he says, "Lord have mercy," every time I mention how Jed and I must get to Pa.

"I have a proposition for you," I say. Oh I am really thinking clearly now. "You need Jed and me to help you get this wagon to Winchester because Samson won't pull it without us."

"And what would *you* be needing?" Roscoe says. From the wagon, Mister Eli starts snoring. I can hear him loud as day.

"Your help getting over the mountain. Four can travel more safely than two. But you must promise you'll put no laudanum in our ginger pop or anything else. You won't hurt Jed or me, nor try to steal our horse."

"I'll do my best, so help me God." Through the darkness between us, Roscoe's gaze settles on mine. I like his eyes. They look honest. "But I can't be swearing for Mister Eli."

"We'll make him swear later. When he wakes up." Maybe we'll be over the mountain by then!

"He's a good man, that Mister Eli," Roscoe says. "I'd do anything for him. He saved my daddy's life—"

"Wait right here!" With Roscoe's loyalty to Mister Eli, I sense I need a Holy Bible Pact to seal Roscoe's pact with *me*. I run over to Jed and retrieve Cousin Ezekiel's Bible from the pack beneath my sleeping brother's head.

Holding out the Bible, I say, "Roscoe, do you know that if you make a solemn vow on a Holy Bible and you break that vow, you could bring on the end of the world with lightning, thunder, earthquakes, hailstones—heavy as a hundredweight, dropped on men from heaven—and plagues of ugly toads and June bugs, too?"

Roscoe says, "I reckon."

"Then put your hand on this Bible and swear everything that you swore earlier to me."

Roscoe does and then he says, "Now you've got to do some swearing, too!" With my hand on the Bible, he says, "What name might you be goin' by for this here pact?"

"You're to call me Adam."

"That ain't your rightful name."

"It is now. And it will be until I get my pa home—so help me God!" I surprise myself by how strongly I feel about this.

"*Adam.* Do you swear to be a kind and faithful traveling companion to Mister Eli, just like I am? Do you swear to get this here Bible horse to pull the wagon in the best way he knows how? Do you swear not to sneak off with him, leaving Mister Eli and me on that wide mountain with only one horse and a sorry one at that?"

"I swear it all, so help me God." This won't be hard. I am generally faithful and always kind—except for once when Jakie Seitz threatened to beat up little Jed. I pushed Jakie to the ground and he . . . he called me a *pismire!* So I punched him in the nose and sat on him until he cried, "Uncle."

But I was only ten at the time. Now, at almost thirteen and having read the entire book on etiquette Pa gave me, I have learned to scorn any behavior that isn't ladylike. Well, that isn't exactly true. But it was until I put on trousers.

"By noon, we should be having rain," Roscoe calls out to me from the wagon seat. I should be sitting on that seat, too, but I have to lead Samson. He won't budge without me because he's scared of nasty Dixie who's hitched beside him. Above our heads, dawn lights the sky a chilly blue with thin gray clouds stretched out across it. It's going to be a long, cold, wet and tiresome day. Worrisome, too, with both Mister Eli to deal with when he finally wakes up and then, that mountain, too.

"You could be warm and toasty dry in this here wagon," Roscoe calls out. "Samson shouldn't need you walking with him step-by-step."

"He seems to think he does." It's hard for Samson to pull a heavy wagon with a nasty partner who'd like nothing better than to sink her yellow teeth into his soft gray flank. Dixie's got her ears pinned back even now—after two hours of teaming up with Samson. He's covered in a nervous sweat.

From the wagon behind us comes a moaning sound. Someone's finally awakening! Is it Jed or Mister Eli? They've been sleeping in the wagon all this time—side by side—and neither one knows the other one's there.

"That sounds like Mister Eli," Roscoe says. He sounds nervous. "You best let me talk to him. I knows how to put things in words he understands."

I hand Cousin Ezekiel's pocket Bible to Roscoe. "You make sure Mister Eli swears to everything I said. *You make him swear.*"

"I'll try." Roscoe gives me an uneasy smile before disappearing into the wagon. I do trust Roscoe. Not only does he have honest eyes, but as we've been traveling together, I've learned that he has a great-grandmother— Mo-ma—who's just like Cousin Ezekiel! She wanders in the woods, preaching about God to all the trees. Roscoe wants to be with his daddy as much as Jed and I want to be with ours. Once this trip to Winchester is over, Roscoe's going north to join his daddy at Camp Meigs in Readville, Massachusetts. Roscoe says he'll march side by side with his brave daddy to set all men of color free and reunite these United States, which I think is a brave and wonderful thing. How did someone as nice as Roscoe team up with Mister Eli?

"Please, Roscoe. Talk softly. My head hurts," I hear him say from the wagon's dim interior.

"Jed and Adam are going with us to Winchester," Roscoe says softly and Mister Eli mumbles, "Dear Lord, how could this have happened? Roscoe, what have you done? What will our good friend Owen say?"

Owen? As in Owen from Cavetown?

"Mister Owen won't say nothin'," Roscoe says. "He likes children. He has eight himself. I explained it all to Adam—sayin' we just be buyin' *shoes* from Owen. Ain't nothin' wrong with buyin' *shoes.*"

I don't hear any answer from Mister Eli.

"Now I done a Holy Bible Pact with Adam," Roscoe just goes right on. "I swears to him we'd be loyal partners and you needs to swear it, too."

"You swore that?" Mister Eli mumbles something I can't make out and then he says, "I won't swear to anything. But, if they insist on joining us, I suppose we could use a few more outlaws in this merry band."

Roscoe chuckles. "Why, yessir, we could, Mister Eli." I reach out and straighten Samson's forelock. *Outlaws?* "They won't give you no trouble," Roscoe continues. "They've got a Bible horse! He's taking them to Winchester to save their dying daddy with boneset tea and Live-forever! But they need us to help them find their way, Mister Eli. And now old Cadwallader is dead and we've got seems like half the country sniffing up our tails, good God almighty, we need them!"

TEN

THE RAIN ROSCOE predicted earlier comes with the afternoon—gray and dismal. My water-proofed poncho keeps me dry from shoulders to knees, but my trouser bottoms—trouser bottoms!—soak up rainwater the way that bread does grease. The wet wool chafes my calves and ankles as I lead Samson through the pounding rain and up the steep mountainside. I think of our Union soldiers marching uphill through mud and rain in their blue wool uniforms. I feel sorry for them. I feel sorry for all of us who must go off to see the elephant in trousers.

Behind me, Mister Eli drives the horses while Jed and Roscoe scout the muddy road ahead for Rebel spies, bloody-minded miscreants and One-Eyed Pete. Mister Eli describes Pete as a rotten, no-good Union Army deserter from somewhere out west. He wears a black patch over one eye, fancy boots with silver spurs that jingle and he carries an extra-fancy rifle with a telescope attached that can shoot you from a hundred yards away. Mister Eli is quite a storyteller!

He claims he bested One-Eyed Pete in a recent business deal and so Pete keeps revenge against Mister Eli burning hot and steady in his heart. Mister Eli says danger from Pete lurks at every curve in the steep mountain road.

"I think you made him up," I told Mister Eli. I could believe that half the country might be out to get him, but not a silver-spurred, black-patched Union Army deserter.

"If only I had." Mister Eli shuddered when he said this, which made my mouth go dry. Could Pete exist?

"Anna! You won't believe what I found!" Jed comes barreling out of the rainy mist ahead. Ever since he awoke from his long night's sleep and found himself traveling with a sutler up a Pennsylvania mountainside, Jed's been so excited he's forgotten important things such as calling me Adam! Again! Being a part of Mister Eli's merry band is a grand adventure for Jed. I haven't told him it's a band of *outlaws* nor that Mister Eli tried to steal our horse. I console myself—*Soon we'll be with Pa.*

"Look at this!" Jed holds up a rusted horseshoe. "It's a Confederate horseshoe! Know how I know? See the initials stamped in the curve—CSA? That's Confederate States of America! A Rebel spy's been in these parts! The enemy's been to Pennsylvania!"

"Is the enemy here now?" I try not to shiver.

"I don't think so. We couldn't find any fresh tracks." Jed sounds almost disappointed. "Roscoe thinks the horse threw the shoe last fall—that time Lee crossed the Potomac."

"Lee had better not cross it again!" I don't know what

I'd do if I should encounter any Rebel invading my home state. I just might throw him to the ground the way I once did Jakie Seitz and sit on him until he sang all five verses of "The Battle Hymn of the Republic."

At nightfall, we set up camp under overlapping hemlock branches deep in a hollow on what Mister Eli has told us is the Maryland side of the mountain. We've crossed the mountain summit. We've made it out of Pennsylvania. We're one state closer to Pa and one state closer to the Rebels. Tomorrow should be mostly downhill.

We tether the tired horses where they can nibble on wet Maryland grass, but we don't tether them near each other. Samson won't let us and I can't blame him. Even now, with her mouth full of grass, that nasty Dixie eyeballs him.

Mister Eli warns us that miscreants such as One-Eyed Pete thrive on cold wet rainy nights and mountain mist. We must continue to be on our guard! Jed, the youngest, will take first watch. Roscoe will take second. I'll take over the third and final watch at three A.M. All we have to do is sit on the wagon seat, look sharp, listen and under no circumstances are we to fall asleep. If anything seems out of the ordinary, we're to shout for Mister Eli, who has a gun.

Now, rubber poncho pulled over his head to keep out the rain, Jed keeps watch while, inside the wagon, Roscoe and I eat biscuits and canned ham. We are crammed between boxes, barrels and stacks of clothes Mister Eli means to sell to his regiment stationed in Winchester—

the 122nd Regiment of Ohio Volunteers. However, Mister Eli not only transports goods clearly meant for soldiers. He also transports goods clearly meant for ladies—the green velvet bonnet he offered to let me wear last night, a green velvet dress to match it and a stack of ladies' hoops! I wonder aloud why a sutler for the Union Army would carry hoops?

"The Winchester ladies ordered them hoops to make their skirts stick out pretty," Roscoe answers for Mister Eli, who is ailing. Seated on a box marked "Peter Stout's Dry Goods," Mister Eli's been silently reading Cousin Ezekiel's Bible; Mister Eli can't eat like the rest of us because of his infected tooth. Earlier, he told me, "If a surgeon carrying his tooth extraction apparatus should appear out of the mist, I would greet him with an open mouth!"

"I didn't know Yankee ladies lived in Winchester," I say now.

"These hoops ain't for Yankee ladies. They're for Rebel ones," Roscoe says, which makes my biscuit stick in my throat. Mister Eli's not supposed to trade with Rebels! They're the enemy! No wonder Mister Eli calls us a band of *outlaws!* No wonder half the country is out to get him!

"Now don't you be thinking nasty thoughts about Mister Eli," Roscoe says. "A good sutler trades with anyone in need. And good God almighty, them Winchester ladies sure think they are in need! General Milroy and our Union Army have taken over their town and them ladies can't get nothin' for themselves or their little children! General Milroy won't let them buy food or dry goods at the stores. He won't let them buy hay or corn to feed their milk cows. He says, 'You and your kin brought on this devilish rebellion! You deserve to starve!' "

"Well that wasn't very nice of General Milroy." I may hate the Rebels, but still, I would never starve women and children.

"Mister Eli, on the other hand, is nice to the ladies and children, too," Roscoe says. "Mister Eli is kind and thoughtful. He brings both sides—Reb and Yank alike—all the things they need."

"Is the velvet bonnet and dress for a Rebel lady?" I ask.

"No indeed." Mister Eli finally speaks. "That dress is for Mrs. Milroy, the Union general's wife." Just saying this seems hard for Mister Eli. He holds his jaw and howls in pain!

"I could make a biscuit poultice for you," I find myself saying as tears well in Mister Eli's eyes. I can't bear to see anyone, even a sutler who trades with the enemy, in such pain. "It'll make that tooth feel better. But I'll need ginger. Do you have ginger?"

Mister Eli nods.

He moans while watching me quickly mash one of my biscuits with rainwater and then add ginger to it. As I reach up to smooth this wet mass on Mister Eli's cheek, he stops my hand. I rest my eyes on his, the way I would with Cousin Ezekiel when he's hurting—*you can trust me*, my eyes say.

Mister Eli nods again. He cups the back of my hand in his. He places my palm that's filled with poultice against his hot and swollen cheek. He holds it there. "That feels good, Nurse Anna," he mumbles.

"No! It's Adam!" No one can remember to call me Adam! But they must!

"Doctor Adam," he mumbles.

No one—not Pa, Cousin Ezekiel or Jed—has ever called me *doctor*. I like the sound of it! Now that I'm Adam, I *could* be a doctor.

When I finish *doctoring* Mister Eli, he covers my hand with his and places my palm on Cousin Ezekiel's Bible. "I swear to you, Adam, I will never again take advantage of your good nature."

I am touched by what he's saying and the old Anna in me believes him with all her heart. However, I've been traveling in the world for almost two days and I am slowly growing into Adam. I am now alert to certain things. Such as the fact that Mister Eli might be swearing mightily, but it's not his hand on that Bible.

It's mine.

ELEVEN

Everything is quiet except for the drip-drip-drip of rain off hemlock branches and Mister Eli's snoring in the wagon above me. He's taken that laudanum again. I hope he hasn't taken too much. He needs to wake up quickly if someone should attack us.

I keep watch from underneath the wagon rather than on the seat. Here I'm sheltered from the rain, I have a wagon wheel for a backrest, and I'm well-hidden. I have armed myself with a sturdy stick. If anyone should try to ambush us, I will use the stick to tap a warning on the wagon floor above and then Mister Eli will leap outside with his gun and protect us all.

To keep my mind off anyone who might be creeping through the hemlocks at this very moment, I silently tell myself the story of "Thumbelina." I am just at the part where an ugly June bug holds a sobbing Thumbelina in his pincers when I hear a soft jingle and the muffled sound of footsteps on hemlock needles. Has someone left the wagon to relieve himself? No, I felt no movement in the wagon above me and the footsteps do sound furtive.

I tap the wagon floor overhead. Then, flattening myself to the ground, I creep around a wagon wheel so that I can get a better look. It's dark and the air is thick with misty rain, but I see two trousered legs, a rifle barrel and fancy tooled leather boots with spurs. Only three yards away.

"Cor, would you look at that," One-Eyed Pete whispers. It has to be Pete. *He's for real.* He takes several steps backward and then turns. Now his boot heels with . . . silver spurs face me. I hear a click. His rifle-barrel snaps downward. He must be loading that fancy telescopic rifle of his. *Where is Mister Eli?* I hear another click. *Is the rifle loaded now?* When Pete turns, will he fire that rifle into the wagon?

Jed's in there!

Silently, I gather my feet beneath me. Shrieking, "Somebody help me!" I hurl myself at Pete! I tackle him at the back of the knees the way I've seen Jakie Seitz do to Robert Freeman in the field behind our school back home. And just like Robert Freeman, One-Eyed Pete pitches forward. Only he's not in a field, he's in a stand of hemlocks. He pitches headfirst into the hard trunk of a hemlock and knocks himself out.

Everyone calls me Adam now. Brave Adam who single-handedly knocked out what Mister Eli now calls "one of the most dastardly villains in history." That Mister Eli. He makes everything sound like an exciting adventure story! I guess it helps him take his mind off his main worry—that troublesome tooth.

It's the middle of the day—cold and drizzly. It's been five hours since we left Pete, tied up back there among the hemlocks with a large bump above the black patch that covers his right eye. Mister Eli took away his rifle, his fancy boots with the silver spurs and his trousers, too. I don't think Pete—or anyone else—will be chasing after us any time soon.

"Adam," Roscoe calls out to me. I love how everyone calls me Adam! "You're walkin' funny! You're sashaying like a girl."

"Well, my feet hurt!" Cousin Ezekiel's old brogans have rubbed my feet raw!

"You've got to walk like a boy!" Jed jumps off the wagon seat. He strides ahead of the horses. "Watch me!" He flings his arms, making his rain-slick poncho swing this way and that. The way he marches reminds me of our New Oxford soldiers when they drilled in Centre Square before going off to join the Pennsylvania volunteers. All Jed needs to complete the picture is a big musket like Pa had.

"I don't like the way you're walking," I yell at my little brother. All I need is for him to become a little soldier in the Union Army. He'd get hurt. I mutter, "I've proved myself as Adam. I'll walk the way I please."

I hobble as I lead Samson downhill through the rain to Owen Glendower and Cavetown, our next stop. A gust of wind blows icy rain into my face. Icy water seeps down into my poncho. I am miserably wet from the tips of my ears to my bloody toes. Will I ever be warm again? I call back to Mister Eli, driving the horses with one hand so that he can hold his swollen cheek with the other, "Does Owen Glendower have a shoe shop?" One with a toasty-warm stove.

"You could call it a shop of sorts," Mister Eli mumbles.

Owen's *shop* turns out to be nothing but a rickety old wagon weighed down by several wooden boxes and hidden inside the entrance to a cave on a wooded hillside overlooking a small cluster of houses—Cavetown. I should have known with an outlaw like Mister Eli there'd be no proper shop. I just bet Mister Eli's doing something illegal—probably buying shoes from Owen to sell to Rebel troops! Oh I can't wait to be free of Mister Eli and with my pa!

Under a high overhanging ledge, Owen sits on a wooden box beside a fire. I shiver as Mister Eli hurries over to greet the large gray-bearded man. I'm so cold! Too cold to try and pass myself off as a boy. Too cold to be anyone but Anna. Owen wheezes as he stands. The cave smells of wood smoke and something familiar I can't pin down.

"Eli! How good to finally see you!" Owen gives Mister Eli a bear hug and Mister Eli says, "Easy now, my friend."

"What's this?" Owen holds Mister Eli at arm's length. "Your cheek's as swollen as a chipmunk's! Another bad tooth?" Mister Eli nods, and Owen says, "Shall I pull it out?"

Mister Eli looks at Owen's large fat hands and says,

"Thank you, but I believe I'll wait. There's a surgeon in Winchester—"

"Bloody surgeons. You'd do well to keep away from them." Owen sweeps his eyes from Jed, to Roscoe, to me. "And who might these ragtag urchins be? I know Roscoe, but I've never met these other two. By God, Eli, where do you find them?"

"Oh here and there." Mister Eli introduces us as Jed and *Adam*. I stiffen when Owen leans closer to inspect me. He'll sense my disguise and I'm too cold to care. I get a whiff of that familiar smell again. *Pig manure*. I glance at Owen's boots. They're slick with pig manure. A longing for home, Cousin Ezekiel and Lauden Honor sweeps over me.

"You're a might pudgy, Adam," Owen says. "I should put you to work on my farm. Carrying slops and cleaning pigpens could slim you down and build up that chest."

My chest?

"I don't think Adam needs building up." Mister Eli steps in for me. What a surprise. He says, "Our Adam took on One-Eyed Pete single-handedly. Adam knocked him out!"

"You don't say!" Owen looks at me in admiration. I didn't really knock out One-Eyed Pete—a tree did—but still. I lift my chin and throw my shoulders back. I smile gratefully at Mister Eli.

"Adam and Jed are on their way to Winchester to join their father," Mister Eli says.

"His name is Abraham, as in Abraham Lincoln," Jed says. "He's been badly wounded. But *Adam* and I will save him." He links arms with mine; we're comrades. I am feeling warmer already.

"Of course you will." Owen tousles Jed's hair. "Just don't say the name *Abraham Lincoln* outside of this cave. You're too close to Jefferson Davis country."

"Jefferson Davis is president of the South," Jed whispers up at me. "He lives in Richmond, the capital."

"I know that, Jed." Why must he always be such a show-off?

"Them Confederates have thrown my Johnny in prison, down there in Richmond," Owen says. His small dark eyes settle on Mister Eli. The two of them exchange an anxious glance. "Into that hellhole, Castle Thunder," Owen says. "They've got him cooped up with the scum of the earth—murderers, thieves and those plug-uglies out of Baltimore."

"I heard tell of Castle Thunder," Roscoe says. His sweet brown eyes have grown so large with fear, my own heartbeat quickens. Castle Thunder sounds like something out of "Thumbelina"—a stone fortress where an ugly toad might hold a princess captive—or worse. "It's a bad place," Roscoe says. "The boss man, Captain Alexander, orders his guards to hang prisoners up by the thumbs! Worse still, that Captain Alexander, he's got a big black dog named Nero. If you breathe too hard, that Nero will bite off your toes!"

"That's enough, Roscoe," Mister Eli says.

"Do Rebels throw wounded Union soldiers into Castle Thunder?" I ask. What if they capture Pa and throw him in that hellhole?

"Castle Thunder is only for civilians like us," Mister Eli says. *Civilians like us?* Mister Eli turns to Owen. "My dear friend, how in heaven's name did your Johnny end up in a place like Castle Thunder?"

"Caught hauling whiskey," Owen says. "Them Rebels claim he was bringing in illegal whiskey for the citizens of Richmond. My Johnny! Why you could fry him in pig fat before he'd sell our fine Northern whiskey to a Rebel! That whiskey they caught him with was meant for Union troops, which, in spite of laws that state to the contrary, our soldiers need.

"I tell you, Eli, those Rebels just itch to throw all of us Yanks in prison. You can't be too careful." Owen shoots a knowing look toward the boxes piled in his wagon. Why? Do those boxes that I'd feared would hold shoes for Rebels contain something far worse?

Do those boxes hold whiskey?

TWELVE I WISH I HAD ON

the pair of soft silver slippers I once saw in Gettysburg at the Leydenberk's shoe shop. They wouldn't hurt my feet. Ever since we left Cavetown two days ago, I've been hobbling along in Cousin Ezekiel's old brogans while leading Samson, who continues to be afraid of Dixie and I can't blame him.

Yesterday, I removed the hated brogans. It felt good to walk barefoot! But then Mister Eli saw my bare feet. Mister Eli said, "Who shall lead us to Winchester if Samson should step upon your toes and break them? I can't bear the thought!" His concern about my feet surprised me—seeing as how he doesn't seem concerned about anything else except his tooth.

"Shoes make the soldier," Mister Eli mumbled as he made me put mine back on. "Without shoes to protect his feet, a soldier might stub his toe and miss a shot. A missed shot could lose a battle. A lost battle could decide the outcome of a war. An entire nation could be lost—all for the want of shoes."

"I never thought shoes were that important," I said.

"They are a highly valued commodity." Mister Eli stared hard at me. "Which is why we must keep the fact that we're transporting Owen Glendower's boxes of *shoes* a secret. We wouldn't want anyone to steal them. Those boxes of *shoes* will fetch a fabulous price in Winchester," Mister Eli said.

In truth, those boxes will fetch a fabulous price anywhere. But it's not because they contain shoes. I am certain those boxes, which Mister Eli had Roscoe and me carefully hide beneath the velvet folds of a dress meant for Mrs. Milroy, a Union general's wife, contain contraband whiskey. Transporting whiskey is against the law—Reb and Yank alike! If we get caught with it . . .

It's raining again. Mister Eli's wagon rolls noisily down the main street of Williamsport, Maryland, in a misty rain. It is here at Williamsport we cross the Potomac River into Virginia. Here we cross that great dividing line between the North and South. Provided we can get safely past our own Union picket line. I hope. Earlier, Mister Eli whispered to me, "If a nosey Yankee picket discovers our boxes of *shoes*, we'll each get twenty lashes with a whip!

"We must be quietly cautious and . . . careful," Mister Eli said.

I can hear him groaning now from the wagon seat behind me while Roscoe, beside him, clucks in sympathy. I can't understand why someone as sweet as Roscoe is so loyal to Mister Eli! He's a crook! Oh why can't he stop that moaning! Mister Eli needs to buckle down and be strong. We must all be strong bricks to get through our Union picket line!

"We must remember what Pa says about the making of bricks," I tell Jed, marching beside me—a brave little soldier. He's preparing himself to cross the Potomac into Rebel country. Unlike me, he doesn't know about the whiskey, which is just as well. "Hot fires make strong bricks, Jed!"

He thrusts out his chin and throws back his shoulders.

"My daddy is a strong brick," Roscoe calls down from the wagon seat. "My daddy done been tested by the fires of hell. His boss man put a red-hot branding iron to my daddy's arm. Brands him with the letter S for *slave*. He says, 'You be nothin' but a dirty slave.'"

I feel myself grow real quiet inside. I've never heard of anyone being branded and I know little of slavery. We never talked about it at home.

"One day, my daddy up and leaves that boss man." Roscoe's eyes rest on mine. I now walk backward so that I can face him. *Roscoe's daddy was branded a slave?* "He runs off to Richmond where he meets up with Mister Eli. Mister Eli packs my daddy in a box two feet eight inches deep, two feet wide and three feet long. My daddy curls himself so tight to fit into that box, he can't barely breathe. That box was marked *shoes,* too!"

"How can you make up a shoe-story about your own daddy?" With Roscoe and Mister Eli, shoes are never only shoes! I turn around. Steep and muddy slopes tower on either side of me. Our road has cut straight through a hill and since I've been walking backward, I hadn't even noticed.

"My shoe-story is as true as rain," Roscoe calls out to me. "Ain't that right, Mister Eli?"

"I nailed up that box myself," he mumbles.

"Mister Eli shipped that box overland express to Mr. Johnson, Arch Street, Philadelphia, Pennsylvania," Roscoe says as I lead Samson across a little canal bridge. "For some time, my brave daddy traveled upside down on his head!" Roscoe calls. "He just kept thinkin', if I can get through this, I'm free. Those railway men, they tossed him about—them, thinking he's just a box of shoes.

"But he made it, and he climbed out a free man and now my daddy is a private in the Union Army! Mister Eli done helped to bring my daddy to a new life."

That explains why Roscoe loves Mister Eli. If he'd saved my pa, I suppose I'd love him, too.

"Are there slaves in Winchester?" Jed asks Roscoe.

"No siree. That General Milroy done freed them all."

"He's a great general." Jed speaks as if he knows the man. Jed's never even met him!

"Well, I wouldn't call General Milroy great," Mister Eli mumbles, "but he does have some good points." I want to ask what he means by this, however my attention is all caught up by what I now see in the mist ahead of me and down a long slope—*the Potomac River.*

The line between the North and South isn't as big as I had imagined—not miles and miles of treacherous water. At this point, the Potomac looks about a hundred and fifty yards wide at most. To think that's all that separates us from those dirty Rebels who want to tear apart our precious nation!

A rope, suspended from high poles, stretches from one bank of the Potomac to the other. A ferry, pulled up on our shore, is attached to this high rope by a long looped rope and pulley. Is this how we're to cross the river into the Rebel state of Virginia? On a ferry? But what about Samson? Beside me, Samson slows his pace.

Five soldiers in blue uniforms lounge around a nearby campfire—*Yankee pickets*. As our wagon bumps over a mix of river sand and gravel toward them, two of the pickets grab their muskets and hurry over to meet us. I want to turn around. I want to run back up the slope we just came down! Beside me, Samson, who's never seen a body of water larger than his friendly Conewago Creek, much less army pickets and a ferry, does what he's inclined to do when he's suddenly surprised. About six yards from the river, he digs his forehooves into the sand, sits down on his hindquarters and snorts.

THIRTEEN "This sittin-

down horse is the strangest sight I ever did see," a Yankee picket says. He looks to be the age of Robert Freeman— only seventeen. The picket seems kind; not at all the type to snoop through a sutler's wagon. He pets Samson's nose while Samson looks down at him in mild surprise. I don't believe Samson's ever seen a man in uniform—excluding Pa.

"Once, I had a plow horse get down to his knees," an- other picket, heavyset with folded arms resting on his belly, says. "He thought he could lie down and nap on me. I popped him right back up. But I never had one sit down. Does he often sit like this?"

"Only when he's contemplating or—scared." If I were a horse, I'd be sitting on my hindquarters right now, too.

Jed looks up in wonder at these two Yankee pickets with their smart blue caps that have brass insignias on them. Jed would just love to be a soldier. The three re- maining pickets saunter over to us. Two stop to talk with Mister Eli and Roscoe and a wide-eyed Jed joins them.

The third picket, skinny and with a hungry look on his face, runs his shifty eyes over Mister Eli's wagon. My heart is pounding in my boy's shirt. This picket looks as if he knows trouble and where to sniff it out. I can't let him snoop through Mister Eli's wagon!

The shifty-eyed picket turns to me. "That's quite a horse you have."

"Samson's a Bible horse! Watch this!" I reach up and scratch Samson's itchy spot, where the heavy black harness collar rubs his neck. He raises his head. I scratch harder. He curls his upper lip inside out. I scratch harder still and he wiggles that lip, as if he's nuzzling the sky. At this key moment, I shout, "Praise the Lord, Samson!"

Samson lets out a whinny that praises the Lord clear across the Potomac River and into Virginia, too. Beside him, Dixie lets out a squeal. The soldiers guffaw. The heavyset one says, "Now don't that beat all."

Samson's loud whinny brings the ferryboat captain clomping down his boat ramp. A big, barrel-chested man with a large nose the purple color of ripe grapes, he carries a whip under his right arm. Is this how he convinces frightened horses to board his ferry? With a whip? He can't whip Samson!

Jed studies the ferryboat captain as he speaks to Mister Eli about the cost of transporting his horses and wagon across the Potomac's treacherous rapids, and the shifty-eyed soldier studies Mister Eli's wagon.

"Now watch this!" I shout. The shifty-eyed picket turns back to me. I tap Samson's nose to get his attention. "How many commandments are there, Samson?" I shout at the old horse.

Samson lowers his head. He stretches out his nose, nuzzles my shirt and snorts.

"That's right!" I say. "You good old Samson!"

"He didn't say nothin'," the shifty-eyed soldier says.

"Yes he did," I say.

"He said ten," Jed calls over to us.

"I distinctly heard ten," Mister Eli calls out clearly even though it must hurt his tooth. He goes on to explain to the shifty-eyed soldier that it's the accent which has him confused. Samson hails from southeastern Pennsylvania where he's picked up a decidedly German accent. This makes everybody laugh. I smile over at Jed. He smiles at me. Mister Eli says, "And now, if all you good soldiers will please excuse us, we have a boat to board." We certainly do!

I shout Samson's favorite passage from the Song of Solomon and he rises majestically to his feet.

"Now that truly is a Bible horse," the heavyset soldier says. The one who reminds me of Robert Freeman says, "Wish I could ride him into battle. He'd keep me safe." Yes, he would.

"Love thy neighbor!" Roscoe shouts at our noble Bible horse. Samson, who always obeys this command to move forward, rolls his eyes at the nearby Potomac and that ferryboat he has to board to cross the river into Virginia. He digs in his forehooves. He's going to sit down again. I shout, "Amen, Brother Samson! Amen!"

Samson remains standing, but he's trembling. Dixie, ears flattened, glares at him. I swat her on the neck. "Stop looking at him like that, Dixie. You're scaring him. Now you just look away. Go on. Look away."

The ferryboat captain, whip in hand, comes over to me and says, "I've handled horses like him before. Let me take care of this."

"We never whip Samson," I say.

"You'd better whip him now." The shifty-eyed soldier leans against a wagon wheel. I wish he'd get away from the wagon! "How else you gonna get him to board the boat? Recite him the Apostles' Creed?" The soldier snorts and then he laughs. "Why don't you sing him a hymn?"

"A hymn? Now that's a fine idea!" I know a hymn that Samson loves and I do, too!

"Follow me! Go along with me!" I yell back at Roscoe, Jed and Mister Eli. Turning Samson, I lead him and Dixie, pulling the wagon, back up the slope we just came down. Samson will need a good running start to board that ferry. Once we've reached the top of the slope and are facing the river again, Roscoe gives Jed and me a leg up on our horse.

"All right." I turn to Mister Eli and Roscoe, on the wagon seat behind Jed and me. "Do you know 'The Battle Hymn of the Republic'?"

"Of course we know it," Mister Eli mumbles.

"It's Chaplain McCabe's favorite hymn," Roscoe says. "He's the chaplain of Mister Eli's regiment and that chaplain sings the 'Battle Hymn' wherever he goes!"

"Well, it's Samson's favorite hymn, too. When Jed and I start singing it, join in. And Mister Eli, even though I know it's going to hurt you, you must sing loudly because you have the best voice of us all."

I've moved Samson up hill and forty yards away from the Potomac. He obeys his command to move forward.

Dixie plods beside him, flicking her ears. She doesn't know what to expect. Neither do I.

About thirty yards from the waiting ferry, Samson slows his pace. I nudge him with my heels. I push him forward with my body weight. Staring straight ahead and not sideways at the watching soldiers, I sing out as loudly as I can: "Mine eyes have seen the glory of the coming of the Lord."

Jed, Roscoe and Mister Eli join in. Mister Eli's tenor voice rings out grandly above us all:

> He is trampling out the vintage where the grapes
>   of wrath are stored;
> He hath loosed the fateful lightning of His terrible
>   swift sword;
> His truth is marching on.
> Glory! Glory hallelujah!
> Glory! Glory hallelujah!
> Glory! Glory hallelujah!
> His truth is marching on.

Samson raises his head. Samson arches his neck. Samson prances proudly forward like some kind of warhorse going into battle.

Mister Eli, Roscoe, Jed and I sing the first three verses of the "Battle Hymn" while a prancing Samson with Dixie pulls the wagon down the hill and across the river flats toward the boat ramp. And suddenly, I feel as if I'm going into battle, too. I'm about to cross the boundary between the North and South! And suddenly, I understand the need for a soldier to sing a battle hymn when he has to face the impossible and he's scared. It makes him proud and brave because it feels as if he's a part of something far bigger than he is.

"Glory! Glory hallelujah!" We sing as we near the boat ramp. "Glory! Glory hallelujah!" The words ring out to the clomp of horseshoes on the wooden planks. On the ferry deck, Samson comes to a trembling standstill. He turns his head this way and that, as if to gather courage from all who now sing what I think must be Samson's favorite verse because it certainly is mine:

> He is sounding forth the trumpet that shall never
>   call retreat,
> He is sifting through the hearts of men before his
>   judgement seat.
> Oh be swift my soul to answer him. Be jubilant
>   my feet.
> Our God is marching on.

And it's not only Jed, Roscoe, Mister Eli and me singing these glorious words for Samson, but also the ferryboat captain and all those Yankee pickets on the retreating Maryland shore.

FOURTEEN CROSSING

the Potomac River on a ferryboat with everybody singing his favorite hymn has brought Samson so much courage. He is full of himself. He prances off the boat and onto the Virginia shore. Standing near a pile of old fishnets, Samson reaches over, nuzzles Dixie's neck and gives that ill-tempered old mare a tender love bite! Dixie squeals, but she doesn't bite Samson back. From that moment on, Samson pulls Mister Eli's wagon with Dixie as a team. Samson doesn't need me beside him.

Hallelujah! I can rest my feet.

At a place called Falling Waters, we set up camp for the night. We tether the two horses near each other and they graze side by side as if they are old friends. Now, in his camp chair, which Roscoe has set up for Mister Eli beside my cooking fire, Mister Eli holds his swollen cheek and tries not to moan as I cook our supper—some crackers that I soaked in water and fry in leftover pork fat. Mister Eli's proud singing of the "Battle Hymn" has jarred something inside his infected tooth. It is really hurting now.

As I flip cracker patties, Roscoe and Jed, who have been whispering together beside the wagon, saunter over and crouch beside me. Roscoe warms his hands over my fire and whispers softly so that Mister Eli can't hear, "Mister Eli hurts so much, he's likely to die from pain if someone don't pull that tooth of his. My hands are just too big. Jed and I were wonderin' if you might give it a try. Jed here says you know how."

"But I've only done it once," I whisper. "And only because the doctor couldn't come. Cousin Ezekiel was beside himself with pain. Pulling his tooth felt like ripping raw chicken meat off the bone." I shudder with the memory.

"But you did get his tooth out," Jed whispers.

"Yes I did. But it's the kind of thing you only do for kin when you have no choice and they're suffering."

"Mister Eli is kin."

"He is not!" I concentrate on flipping my cracker patties so that I won't have to look at Mister Eli.

Jed says through his teeth, "Yes he is! That ferryboat captain asked if you and I had official passes to get through the Union lines, which we don't. Mister Eli claimed we didn't need passes; we were his brothers! He made us his brothers so that we could cross the Potomac to save our pa's life, *Adam*."

"Well I never heard anything about this." I look up at Mister Eli. He's staring at my hands. Jed says, "Mister Eli *is* kin."

"I'm no doctor."

"I've been watching your hands," Mister Eli mumbles to me. He's been listening in on everything we've said! "You have such small capable hands. I do believe you *could* be a doctor. *Doctor Adam.*" He tries to smile.

"But I'm afraid to pull your tooth," I say.

"I'm afraid to have you pull it. But dear Adam," he says. "*Doctor Adam.* What choice do *we* have?"

Mister Eli looks up at me from his camp chair, which Roscoe has placed near a cheerful stream that further on turns into a waterfall, tumbling willy-nilly downhill to the gray Potomac. It seems to me I'm riding that stream—being hurtled into doing all sorts of impossible things.

"I'm ready." Jed runs over to us with the packet of wet tea leaves that I asked him to fetch. Once the tooth is pulled, we'll put the packet on Mister Eli's empty socket to draw out the pus and blood because that's what we did for Cousin Ezekiel and it worked.

"I'm ready, too. How's about you, Mister Eli?" Roscoe peers down into Mister Eli's face.

"Ready as I'll ever be." Mister Eli opens his mouth and I lay a wooden stick across his back teeth. He suggested I do this. That way, if pain should drive Mister Eli beyond control, he'll bite down on the stick instead of me. He leans his head back until it rests against Roscoe's sturdy body. With his large hands, Roscoe cradles Mister Eli's head.

Roscoe and Jed now look to me. Jed must sense how anxious I am; he starts to hum the glorious "Battle Hymn." I peer into Mister Eli's mouth; I see no glory here. Only a rotten tooth with a red swollen gum. I smell the whiskey Mister Eli drank to numb himself and, beneath that, rotting teeth.

"I'll wiggle the tooth first," I say. "It'll loosen things

up. Then I'll give a sharp pull sideways, the tooth will pop out and we'll be done."

"I don't remember it being that easy," Jed says. "With Cousin Ezekiel, you had to—"

"Shush, Jed." All Mister Eli needs to hear is how hard and long I had to tug! With a small piece of cotton cloth to give me a grip, I take hold of the rotten tooth. As I wiggle it, Mister Eli's head moves back and forth. His eyes are closed. His hands are clenched. He's preparing himself to die.

"Hold his head firm," I tell Roscoe.

"You be careful with Mister Eli," Roscoe says.

I wiggle the tooth while Jed and Roscoe hum the "Battle Hymn." The longer they hum, the harder I wiggle and the looser the tooth gets. Tears stream out of Mister Eli's closed eyes.

With Cousin Ezekiel, my fingertips sensed when it was time to pull the tooth. It came after considerable tearing. I feel that tearing now. I can't do this. I look away. The moon has come out. That laughing moon shines down on us all. For a moment, I stand outside myself. I see a girl in trousers trying to pull out a sutler's tooth while his good friend Roscoe holds his head and helpful Jed stands nearby with tea leaves.

Are we a team—like Samson and Dixie? We are! And I'm the doctor! I'll pull this tooth. And then, I'll go on to find my pa and save his life. My fingertips clamp down on Mister Eli's tooth. They yank it sharply sideways. Mister Eli's gum splits open like a rotten melon and out comes that stinky tooth—pop.

FIFTEEN WE'RE TRAVELING

southward through the Shenandoah Valley to Winchester. Hills, turning green in the late April sunshine, rise on either side of us. We're in Rebel country but I don't see any Rebel soldiers or one of those she-devils, either. Roscoe says they've all gone into hiding because the Union Army has control of the valley—at least for now.

The first Rebels we do come upon are chickens. Our wagon passes three laughing Union soldiers with live Rebel chickens caught up in their arms. Seems the soldiers stole these little brown chickens from a farmwife. Jed looks up at the soldiers with such admiration. Once they're out of hearing, I remind my little brother that stealing chickens, even Rebel chickens, is wrong. Jed doesn't answer. He just shifts the big stick he now carries as a pretend rifle from one shoulder to the other and marches on.

Outside a small village called Darkesville, a Union cavalry officer reins in his horse. He warns Roscoe, Jed, Mister Eli and me that the Rebel cavalry is on the move.

They've burned bridges to the west of the valley. They've torn up railroad tracks. The Union officer says that even on the well-traveled Great Wagon Road we're following we should be on the lookout for these Rebels and their generals—John D. Imboden and Grumble Jones.

"What do these generals look like?" I need to keep my eyes wide open for them.

"Well son, they'll be wearing gray uniforms. That's a fact," the officer tells me. "I imagine they'll have fancy epaulettes on their shoulders. They'll be sitting tall in their saddles. Those Rebels know how to ride."

"As do our Yankees." Mister Eli smiles at this Yankee officer who, to my mind, doesn't seem to know how to ride. He stands in his stirrups as if his bottom is too sore to sit down on. "You look a bit uncomfortable," Mister Eli says. "I have something that might help you."

He disappears into his wagon and returns with a container of Piercey's Patent Pile Pipes, which are not the kind of pipes you smoke. They are a medicine for rear ends suffering from piles and that's all I know. Mister Eli says, "It's guaranteed to bring relief and it only costs two dollars."

"Two dollars? For that rotgut? That's highway robbery!" With a look of disgust, the officer, still standing in his stirrups, wheels his horse.

"With a little persuasion, I might lower the price," Mister Eli offers.

"I don't have the time of day to persuade a fair price out of a sutler," the officer says. "If I did, I'd spend it seeing that all you sutlers were sent back north to the dark holes you crawled out of. With your inflated prices and conniving ways, you're a disgrace to the Union." With that, he spurs his horse and gallops off, his rear end held high.

"Ah well, one customer's loss will be another's gain." Mister Eli grins at us. I like his cheerfulness. He has become quite cheerful since I pulled out his tooth. I imagine the Yankee officer would be cheerful, too, if he'd treat those piles of his. He should just put aside his ill-feelings about sutlers and learn to live with them. I have. I wonder what Pa would think of Mister Eli and Roscoe? I can't wait to be with Pa.

As we draw nearer to Winchester, we come upon Union pickets. Mister Eli gives them cigars to keep them occupied and away from his wagon with its boxes marked *shoes*. As they light these cigars, the pickets warn us about Rebel bushwhackers who hide out in nearby mountain caves and hollows. This makes me grow more and more frightened about Rebels and so I say to myself a litany Pa once taught me about how hot fires make strong bricks.

With stick-rifle at the ready, Jed marches alongside Mister Eli's wagon. Jed's prepared to protect us all from Rebel bushwhackers with a stick! Mister Eli leads us in singing songs to keep us marching steadily onward to Winchester—"Glory! Glory hallelujah! As we go marching on . . ."

We see no Rebel bushwhackers although Jed's sure they must be out there and every so often I feel a cold stare on my back that makes my skin crawl. We don't see any trees, fences, barns, smokehouses or pigpens either. Since the Union Army has occupied this area for close to four months, the soldiers here have had to tear down almost everything they can find for firewood. We pass one forlorn tree stump after another. Field after fenceless field.

The first real Rebel we encounter, we see only through a drizzly rain and from a distance. Roscoe points this Rebel out to me. "Look! That there's a Rebel she-devil—most likely."

Dressed all in black, this *she-devil* herds several cows through a rain-soaked field that has no fence. She looks thin and smaller than I'd imagined a she-devil would be and she has no horns. She calls out to the cows—"Get along, now Sadie. Lucy-Bird, you move on now. Supper's waiting."

Like several other farms we've passed, her farm has no barn, no outbuilding of any kind, just some stone foundations sticking out of the tall wet grass. The she-devil herds her cows around these stone remains and toward a white house whose windows have been broken and now are stuffed with oil cans to keep out the rain. Its partially opened front door hangs by a single hinge. One by one, the cows amble through that door and into the house, followed by the she-devil.

"Do you think Pa's in there?" Jed slips his hand in mine.

"I hope not, Jed." This place makes me shiver.

"Stanley Bemis will lead us to Pa," Jed says. "As soon as we get to the Union encampment, we'll find Stanley." Jed turns his collar up against the chilly rain and so do I.

We travel through the wet and forlorn streets of Winchester on our way to the Union encampment, just to the west of town. I know that Rebels who aren't off fighting in the army—old men, women and children—live here in Winchester and that the houses we pass are said to harbor bushwhackers. But all I see are soldiers dressed in Union blue. They march in formation down the rain-swept street. Two stand guard at a mansion that has a Union flag hanging over its front door. Soldiers, their rifles propped against a pillar, lounge on the front porch of a big hotel we pass.

These soldiers will protect us.

Walking beside Samson, I slip on the slick wet cobbled street and tumble onto my rear end. As I grab Samson's traces to pull myself back up on my feet, I see a face pressed against the lower-story window in a snug brick house only a stone's throw away. Why it's a little Rebel girl with dark hair, curly the way mine once was. She is smiling at me. I can't help but smile at her and she . . . she waves back.

SIXTEEN WE'RE FINALLY

at the Union encampment with its hundreds of rows of tents and soldiers marching even in the rain. All I want is to find my pa. I can't wait a minute longer to be with him, but Stanley Bemis, who has the same red cheeks as his aunt—our busybody neighbor, Miss Bemis—doesn't seem to want to talk with Mister Eli, Jed and me. Feet propped on a sheet iron camp stove inside a canvas tent that holds a dozen other men, Stanley leans back in his canvas chair to scowl at us over the wire rims of his reading glasses. We've interrupted Stanley's reading.

"Jed and Adam have traveled over a hundred miles to be with their dear father," Mister Eli is saying. "They believe you know where to find him."

"Do they now?" Stanley sniffs his pompous nose. I never liked him; I never will.

"He's from New Oxford, Pennsylvania," I say. "His name is Abraham Sunday."

"*Abraham Sunday?*" Stanley takes off his glasses, puts his feet on the ground and leans forward to peer closely at

Jed and me. Once his eyes fix on me, he stares and stares. "Good God," he finally says, "is that you, Anna Sunday?"

My face turns red hot.

"Her name's Adam," Jed whispers. "She's a boy."

"Good God!" Stanley says. The other men look up from the letters they're writing, the books they're reading and the cards they're playing to stare at me, too.

"It's safer." I force myself to look directly into Stanley Bemis's squinty eyes. "Being a boy in Rebel country."

"But this isn't Rebel country. *This* is General Milroy's country." I can tell by Stanley's tone that he enjoys correcting me. *The toad.* "It's been under General Milroy's control for over four months. We intend to keep it that way. Right boys?"

"That's right," a mustached soldier who's been playing cards says. "Them Rebels might *think* they can take Winchester back. Their she-devils living here *think* their boys can. But we ain't gonna let them."

"No sir, we ain't," a third soldier says.

"We're not here to discuss the Rebels." Mister Eli clears his throat. "Can anyone tell my two young friends where they can find their father?"

"He's . . ." Stanley shakes his head, as if to clear his mind of troubled thoughts. *Do these thoughts have to do with Pa?* "He's . . . at *Faraway.* It's the closest place we could take him after he'd been shot. It's . . . within the Union picket lines." Stanley sounds as if he's apologizing for something. "I do manage to check on him every few days. Your pa . . ." Stanley's trying to find words to describe something bad. I know the signs. I am starting to feel sick.

"We didn't think he'd survive this long," Stanley finally says.

"What's wrong with him?" I say.

"They finally had to amputate his right foot, because of the pus, you see. And now, well, pyemic infection has set in." *Pyemic infection?* I draw close to Jed and he grabs my hand. "He's had chills and fever," Stanley says, ". . . he's been in a delirium for the past three days. I am sorry, Anna."

Stanley's horse jogs nervously alongside Mister Eli, Jed and me. The horse's hooves fling up mud as we make our way through the Union encampment and over to Mister Eli's tent so that Jed and I can get Samson and go to Pa.

I want to be with Pa.

Outside a large tent full of laughing soldiers, a short bearded soldier in a rubber poncho and wearing a tall top hat holds up a cigar he's smoking and calls out, "Mister Eli! Did you get those shoes I ordered?"

"Lieutenant Schmidt! I most certainly did!" Mister Eli smiles at the lieutenant, then turns to Jed and me. "My dear friends. I have an important business matter to attend to here. Will you excuse me?" He winks at us, then looks up at Stanley. "I have an order of fine shoes to sell to the cream of the Union Army! After that, I have another urgent business appointment with the general's wife— Mrs. Milroy. She's ordered the most exquisite dress."

"You won't be selling any dress to Mrs. Milroy," Stanley calls down to him. "She left yesterday for her home in Indiana. She won't be coming back."

Mister Eli looks so disappointed. Here that green velvet dress came all the way from Paris, France, for Mrs. Milroy and now, she isn't here to pay for it. He shakes his head and sighs.

"One customer's loss is another's gain," I remind him.

"Indeed it is." Mister Eli smiles softly at me. "Dear brother Adam. I will miss you."

"I'll miss you, too." I have grown to like being a part of Mister Eli's merry band.

"Your father's a fortunate man—having such loyal children." Mister Eli touches my shoulder and then tousles Jed's hair. "We'll see each other again. We'll eat smoked oysters, roast pork and we'll drink ginger pop. And if you should come upon a fine lady in need of an evening gown . . ."

"We'll send her to you," we both say with tears in our eyes.

When it comes time to bid goodbye to Roscoe, I feel so sad, tears roll down my cheeks no matter how hard I sniff and try to hold them back.

"Now you tell your pa that my grandpappy lost his foot to a bear trap," Roscoe says after helping Jed and teary-eyed me mount Samson with our packs. "My grandpappy hopped around on one foot for his last thirty years. He do just fine. And if you return to this here camp, you be sure to check on Mister Eli. I'll be worried about him, seeing as how I won't be around to help him."

"You're leaving Winchester?" I ask. Leaving Mister Eli?

"I'm leaving for Camp Meigs tomorrow. I'll be traveling with one of Mister Eli's officer friends clear the way to Massachusetts. Think on it," he says as Stanley gestures at us that *we have to go*. "Soon I'll be with my daddy just like you'll be with yours."

PART THREE

Faraway

SEVENTEEN HEAD

lowered, trotting through rain, Samson follows Stanley's horse toward the she-devil's place called Faraway. It's south of the Union camp and hidden deep among the hills. We pass clusters of houses with their curtains drawn and then, one overgrown farm after another. After several miles, Stanley points to a mist-shrouded hill ahead. "Her farm's there. Just over the ridge." A cow moos, sounding lost and lonely. A forested mountain looms in the gray distance off to our left. I shiver in spite of Samson's warmth beneath me. I ask Stanley, "What was Pa doing way out here?"

"Searching farms for Rebel spies." He shifts in his saddle and looks over at me from under the wide-brimmed hat he wears. "These hills are infested with them."

Behind me, Jed gives a sharp intake of breath. My soldier brother must think he's got his work cut out for him now! Oh why must Pa be way out here? Stanley says, "If your pa had stuck with sniffing out spies, he wouldn't have got shot. But no. Your pa had to chase a pig. A soldier left a gate open and a pig escaped. The farmwife started shrieking; your pa shouted, 'I'll catch your pig!'

"He chased that fool pig over a snow-covered hill and out of our sight. There was no stopping him! The next time we saw him, he was lying unconscious in the arms of that she-devil he's staying with now—that Mrs. McDowell. Why he had to chase a pig, I'll never understand."

"Pa's kind. He felt sorry for that farmwife," I say.

"That farmwife is a Rebel sympathizer. The meat from her pig will fill Rebel bellies. Your pa's a fool."

"My pa's no fool!" He's the kindest man I know.

The bright sound of a trumpet comes from the direction of the she-devil's house. The trumpet is playing a sprightly tune I've never before heard—*dump, da-dump, da-da-da.* Samson perks up his ears and breaks into a jog.

"It's that infernal McDowell boy—with that fancy newfangled trumpet of his," Stanley mutters as we come out of a foggy dip in the road and onto the flat crest of a hill. "He has the nerve, playing 'The Bonnie Blue Flag' with Yankee pickets camped in the woods nearby."

"What's 'The Bonnie Blue Flag'?" Jed asks.

Stanley stares at him. "Don't you know?" Stanley stares at me. "Don't either of you know? Dear God, you are babes in the woods! 'The Bonnie Blue Flag' is the rallying cry for Southern independence."

Dump. Da-dump. Da-da-da. Dump. Da-dump. Da-da. The *infernal McDowell boy* continues to play the rallying cry while Samson prances in time to it. He follows Stanley's horse down a dirt lane that runs through a long dark tunnel of apple trees. Halfway down this lane, Stanley calls back to me, "The she-devil considers herself South-ern gentry. Don't let on that you're a girl who's disgraced us all by donning trousers."

"I won't." I'll be Adam until I get my pa safely out of here. So help me God!

A big stone house with three chimneys and five white pillars stands at the end of the she-devil's long lane. Pa's been staying in this house? Is my pa still alive?

In the front yard, the *infernal McDowell boy* plays his fancy trumpet beneath a dogwood tree covered in white blossoms. He has curly golden hair and he is barefoot. He lowers his trumpet when he sees us. He has an aquiline nose! According to all the stories my ma ever told me, an aquiline nose belongs to princes and kings. Here's a Rebel farm boy with one.

Behind him, a small woman dressed in black comes out of the house. A big brown, black and yellow-haired dog trots after her. Seeing us, the dog races across the front yard. It stops at the edge of the grass and barks loudly at us. Samson comes to a sudden halt and does what he's inclined to do when he's surprised. He sits down on his hindquarters to ponder—*well, what do we have here?*

Jed and I do what we're inclined to do under these cir-cumstances. We tumble off. Before I can get to my feet, the dog barrels into me. It knocks me flat and slobbers my face with kisses.

"Joshua McDowell. Get Eggs 'n Bacon off that child this instant!" I hear the woman say.

"Yes, Grandmother." Joshua doesn't sound too happy about doing this. I think he enjoys seeing me flattened in mud. To be truthful, I don't mind all that much. I have missed being loved like this. And I miss Eggs 'n Bacon's kisses as soon as Joshua pulls her off me.

Joshua has the bluest eyes.

Unlike his grandmother's. The she-devil's pale green eyes are taking in my dirty clothes. Does she sense something peculiar about me? Her iron gray hair's pulled fiercely back and tied into a bun. She's thin-lipped, sharp-eyed and looks full of fire for being as old as she is—a grandmother. She turns her sharp eyes from me to Samson, still sitting on his hindquarters while Eggs 'n Bacon sniffs noses with him.

"That's an odd horse," she says. She turns to Stanley who's dismounted in the normal way. "And who might these two children be?"

"This is Jed." Stanley puts a hand on Jed's shoulder. "And this"—Stanley curls up his nostrils in obvious distaste—"is Adam. They've come to see Abraham Sunday, their father."

"I see." The she-devil stares at me—long and hard. Did Pa tell her about his two children—Jed and *Anna* Sunday? Sudden, fierce tears flood her eyes. She says, "You've come a long way." She takes a deep breath, turns to Joshua and says, "Mind the two horses, will you my dear?" To us she says, "Come with me."

She lifts her long hoopskirt to carefully make her way across the muddy yard. I follow her at a distance. She sidesteps a cow patty. "Manure! Cow manure in my front yard!" she fires at Stanley. "I used to have fences to keep Vidalia in her place—until your Yankee pickets burned them down.

"I suppose I should be grateful I still have my barn and house," the she-devil says. "But you couldn't use them for firewood, now could you? They're made from fine Southern stone."

"We could have used that stone to build a fine Yankee fort," Stanley says.

"You wouldn't dare." She stops dead. She only reaches Stanley's chest. Will she take on Stanley Bemis? Has she been kind to Pa? I hope she has. I sidestep her. I climb five stone steps, cross the porch and walk through the large front door she's left open. A smell that reminds me of Mister Eli's rotten tooth sends me reeling. *Pa?*

My footsteps echo off the front hall's wooden floor. I turn left at the stairs that rise in front of me. The parlor door is open. In the dimly lit room, I see someone lying on a cot set up by the fire.

That someone lies so still. He's covered by a gray wool blanket and he sleeps, curled on his left side. I see a hollow where his right foot should be. *He has no foot.* It's only when I stand silently near him that I can tell that he is breathing. But this isn't Pa. My pa's big and strong. My pa would sense my presence and open his eyes.

It is Pa. Up close, I see the bump between his eyebrows he calls his third eye. In the pale light, his hollowed cheeks take on a yellow glow. He has no brick-red beard! SOMEONE HAS SHAVED OFF HIS BEARD!

"Oh Pa, what have they done to you?" I kneel beside him. I take his hot hand in mine. My throat aches so much I can barely speak. "It's your daughter, Pa. It's Anna."

He opens his eyes. Dazed by fever, they search mine.

Does he recognize me? I wish he'd speak. *Say something, Pa.* He takes my hand. He places my hand against his clean-shaven cheek and shuts his eyes.

I kneel beside him. Laying my head gently against his chest the way that Thumbelina did with a dying swallow in a faraway place called "Once Upon a Time," I listen to the rhythm of my dear pa's shallow breathing. Through my tears, I whisper to him over and over again, "You're alive. You're alive. You're alive."

EIGHTEEN

My pa has always been the strongest man in all of New Oxford. He can carry logs bigger around than Miss Bemis's pet pig, Charity. He can split these logs faster than any man alive and keep the kiln fires at Mr. Alwine's brickyard burning night and day. People often marvel at my pa's strength. They ask him, "What's your secret?" He winks at them and says, "It's all in the beard."

Cousin Ezekiel warned Pa to guard his magnificent beard. Didn't Samson, who was the strongest man alive, lose his strength when Delilah, the Philistine, came along and shaved his head? "Beware of women who carry razors," Cousin Ezekiel said.

Mrs. McDowell is not only a she-devil, but a Delilah and a Philistine, too! She's been shaving my pa daily with a razor that belonged to her late husband, Angus McDowell, a noted lawyer and collector of rocks! How can my pa ever get well now? *He only has one foot.*

"Oh stop fussing," she tells Jed and me after I'd lashed out at her for shaving Pa. We are in her late husband's study and through the open door we can see Pa, curled like a caterpillar on his cot and with that one foot gone. "Don't be such ninnies! No man's strength is in his beard!" She turns to Stanley. "I had to shave Abraham. That useless Private Hardin let food dribble onto his face and his beard became so soiled and matted, I feared it would cause sores. I have enough worries without worrying about sores."

"You shouldn't be worrying about Abraham," Stanley says while Pa lays there deadlike on his cot. "He's no concern of yours. Where's Private Hardin?"

"He's where I sent those other two nincompoops you said would nurse Abraham. Out back cleaning the chicken coop. It's all he's good for. All any of you Yankees are good for.

"Except, of course, for Abraham." In a softer voice, she tells Jed and me that, even though our pa is a Yankee, he is no nincompoop. He is a good and gentle man who got shot when he was only trying to catch a pig. That pig, we learn, is Miss Adelaide's prized boar, Patrick Henry. Miss Adelaide is Joshua's maiden aunt and Mrs. McDowell's neighbor. "She's a kind and simple soul," Mrs. McDowell says. "Your father, unlike the other Yankee soldiers, treated her with respect. For that alone, I'd do anything to save him. And now that you're here, you can help me."

I find it surprising that a Rebel she-devil is so determined to save a Yankee soldier. I wonder about it. "I'll take over Pa's care," I tell her. "I'll feed him. I'll wash his face. As his beard grows in, I'll groom it."

"I'll take care of Pa, too," Jed says, which is quite brave

of him. Jed may be good at going on journeys and collecting facts and scouting the road ahead, but he's never comfortable around the sick. He's too rutchety.

"We'll get your father over this dreadful infection," Mrs. McDowell says gently to Jed. *We?* She's going to help us?

"How will he walk with just one foot?" Jed's voice has gone all high-pitched. He's troubled over Pa's missing foot. I am, too.

"With crutches, Jed." Those fierce tears are in Mrs. McDowell's eyes again. She seems to care about Pa. Really care. She seems good and kind and to love Pa. She says, "And then all you Sundays can return home to Pennsylvania where you belong." Which makes me wonder about her all over again.

She says until we can go home, Samson may stay in her barn. She has more than enough room for him—seeing as how the Yankees have stolen every single horse she had. Jed and I may stay in the study. It's light and roomy. As for Private Hardin? She tells Stanley, "That nincompoop can return to the Union camp with you; I have no room for him here."

"He'll stay out back in the slaves' cabin," Stanley says.

"You mean the servants' cabin, Private Bemis." She draws herself up. For a moment, I think she's going to spit in Stanley's eye. I almost hope she will. She says, "I have never kept slaves; I never will. I believe in freedom and in the holy cause of states' rights—a concept you and your tyrannical government have trouble grasping."

"Private Hardin stays at Faraway." Stanley glares at her. She glares right back. After several uncomfortable moments she says, "All right. He can take over the night watch. That way I won't have to look at him."

For a grandmother, this she-devil has what Cousin Ezekiel would call a lot of spirit.

Soon after this, Stanley tells Jed and me there are duties he must attend to back at camp. He's unsure when or if he'll be coming back to Faraway. He makes a point of taking Jed and me out back to the chicken coop to introduce us to Private Hardin, who's here to represent the Union Army, keep us safe and take care of Pa's needs.

Private Hardin doesn't look as if he can take care of anyone's needs. Old and bent, Private Hardin reminds me of a pretzel topped by thin gray hair and his teeth are stained an ugly brown from chewing tobacco. He spits tobacco juice at a poor little one-eyed chicken—startling her out of her nest. He says to Jed and me, "You sure came a long way to tend to a dying man."

I answer calmly, though my heart is in my throat, "We came to bring our pa back from the dead and we will." Nothing will stop us! Not the Rebel spies in these infested hills. Not even a nincompoop like you!

While Jed unpacks our belongings in the study, I prop Pa up so that Mrs. McDowell can spoon-feed him his medications. To help Pa get over his pyemic infection, Dr. Beck, the Union Army surgeon, has put Pa on a strict regimen of brandy, quinine and sesquichloroid, which he must be given every two hours. He stares bleary-eyed at the parlor fire while the brandy Mrs. McDowell has given him dribbles out of his mouth and onto his chin. Pa shows

no sign that he's even aware that it's me, his Anna, holding him.

As I wipe his face, Pa's blanket slips off. Even though
I know he has no foot, still, I'm startled when I see that
blank space where his foot should be. A yellowed and
crusty-looking bandage covers the stump. Oh I can't bear
to look at this. Mrs. McDowell says, "We'll need to
change that."

I try to be brave. I nod.

"It's hard to tend to injured kin." Mrs. McDowell re-
arranges Pa's blanket so that it covers his bandaged leg.
She helps me to lay him down on his left side. "It takes a
special someone to handle it. Someone like an Anna Sunday, who has cut off her hair and put on trousers."

"You know." Now she's going to scold me.

"Of course I know." She touches my cheek. "You're a
brave girl. I wonder if, in your situation, I could be so
brave.

"Abraham has spoken lovingly of you."

"Please don't tell anyone I'm a girl." I need to stay a
boy. It's safer.

"I won't tell anyone. It will be our secret." She smiles
gently at me.

"I don't make a very good boy," I confide. "I can do
certain things quite well, but I can't seem to walk the right
way."

"I'd be proud to walk in your footsteps," she says.

"I won't change back. Not yet." I want her to understand this. "I need to stay Adam until I get Pa home. I
vowed this on the Holy Bible—so help me God!"

"Then we'd better get your father well quickly," Mrs. McDowell says. "For I sense a strong girl inside your loving heart. We wouldn't want her trapped inside there forever." She pats my hand and something about her warmth and understanding makes me burst into tears. Without thinking, I throw myself into Mrs. McDowell's arms. And even though she's a Rebel she-devil and I'm a Yankee and we don't know each other all that well, she hugs me close and I let her hug me as I cry and cry.

NINETEEN

Hardin sits with Pa now. He's so thin that, from here in the study, I can't make him out beneath his gray blanket. I am so afraid my pa will die. How can I keep my pa from dying?

In a glow of lamplight, Mrs. McDowell's late husband's rocks and crystals glitter down at me from their high shelves. As I slowly unpack my belongings, Jed reads a book about rocks he found on a study shelf. The old house around us creaks. Someone walks across the floorboards overhead. Someone's dragging something.

Jed puts aside his book. The dragging noise continues. Jed whispers, "That sounds like a dead body being dragged across the floor."

"Don't be silly," I whisper. Something thumpety-thumps down the stairs.

"It's a dead Union soldier's body. Joshua's trying to hide it somewhere we can't see." Something swishes across the hall floor. Jed's voice grows more hushed. "That Joshua is dangerous. He's a Rebel spy."

"What makes you say that?" I whisper.

"He played 'The Bonnie Blue Flag' as we came riding up his lane. That was a signal to his bushwhacker friends—watch out, the Yanks are coming." The dragging noise enters the parlor. Jed creeps over to me. We peek in. But it's not a dead body being dragged into the parlor! It's two straw ticks! Joshua McDowell drags in two straw ticks—mattresses for Jed and me to sleep on!

"Jed Sunday! You're a fool!" Just because the McDowells are Rebels, Jed suspects the worst of them! He never suspected anything bad about Mister Eli, who was a crook! Jed just shrugs.

Joshua stops and he bends over Pa. I hear Joshua say, "Private Sunday. Your two young 'uns have come to take you home. You're going to get well and go home, you hear?"

"He's too close to dead to hear," Private Hardin says, which brings tears to my eyes. That Joshua, he turns his back on Private Hardin. Joshua drags the ticks into the study and I pretend to be looking at Angus McDowell's rocks while wiping away my tears.

"Those rocks were put up high to keep them out of Eggs 'n Bacon's reach," Joshua says. "That dog just loves to steal those rocks, sneak on down to the millpond and drop them in.

"She throws a conniption fit when they disappear into the water," he says. Averting my eyes—I don't want him to sense how sad I am—I help Joshua lay the ticks out side by side while Jed pretends to read his rock book. Jed wants nothing to do with a *Rebel spy*.

"If you hear Eggs 'n Bacon barking as if it's the end of the world, you'll know she's gone and lost another of Grandfather's rocks," Joshua says. "She's already lost two of his prized geodes. Ever seen a geode?"

From one of the high shelves, Joshua removes a gray rock about the size and shape of a goose egg and tosses it over to me. "That there could be a geode; its insides full of sparkling crystals," he says while I turn it over in my hands. The surface is rough and pitted with scars. "Then again, it might be an ordinary rock—solid and ugly clear the way through."

"It looks like an ugly old rock to me," Jed calls out.

"Well let's crack it open and find out!" Joshua puts the egg-shaped rock into a sock I've just unpacked. He retrieves a hammer from his grandfather's desk and places the rock-filled sock on the study's wooden floor. Jed draws close. He's as fascinated as I am. I'm glad Joshua came in here.

"Now watch this!" He raises the hammer high above his head and smashes it so hard upon the rock-filled sock, something breaks. The floor beneath it? Did he break the floor? Joshua picks up the sock with the smashed rock inside. There's a huge pockmark on the floor beneath it. He notices my noticing. He says, "Grandmother would go hog-wild if she saw that. But we won't tell her."

What Joshua brings out of the sock drives away any worry I might have. "It *is* a geode," he says. He hands us the broken halves of rock—one to me, the other to Jed. The geode halves look like nests of sparkling stars.

"These are quartz crystals." Joshua traces the starry

insides of the geode I am holding in my hand. Joshua's being kind—showing me stars when, in the next room, someone near to me is dying. "Ain't they pretty?" Joshua says. "See how they had to grow inward, toward the geode's heart? That's because there was no other place for them to grow."

I can understand how this could happen, being a sort of geode myself. Inside, I'm a girl named Anna who's beginning to think that she likes Joshua. *He's so kind.* But I must push any warm feeling for him deep inside my heart. Because on the outside, I am a Yankee boy.

And Joshua—he's a Rebel!

There are two rules us Yankees living in a Rebel house must obey. Mrs. McDowell laid them down for us this rainy morning after I helped her give Pa his medications and a cup of beef tea, which he refused to drink. Mrs. McDowell's first rule is that Joshua is not allowed to break open any more rocks for us. There are now only *two* possible geodes left to be passed on for future generations of McDowells to ponder and break open should they desire. Joshua was wrong to have opened the third of these mysteries and he damaged a floor in the process! However, under the circumstances—he said he did it to cheer us up—it will be overlooked.

Secondly, there are certain areas in a Rebel household that are off-limits to Yankees of any shape or size. There is Mrs. McDowell's bedroom at the top of the stairs and to our right. It has red-flowered wallpaper, a window that overlooks the rain-splattered front yard with its dogwood, a washstand with a white pitcher and bowl and one of the largest beds I have ever seen. "My late husband was a tall man," Mrs. McDowell explains as she shows us this room where we are not allowed. "He stood six feet four inches high."

"That's the same height as Abraham Lincoln," Jed says proudly and without thinking.

"It's because of your Abraham Lincoln that I have had to resort to this." Mrs. McDowell reaches under her pillow and brings out a pearl-handled pistol, which makes Jed's and my eyes grow big. She holds the gun up so that we can see it clearly. I can tell by the steady way Mrs. McDowell handles the gun and the steely look that has come over her green eyes, she knows how to fire it. She says, "Never enter my room without first knocking and announcing your name. Otherwise, I might think you're some half-crazed Yankee out to attack me. I might shoot you.

"Lord knows," she says as Jed elbows me and a pained look crosses her face, "I would never want to shoot you."

Next, there's the garret. Mrs. McDowell doesn't take us up there because, she says, it holds nothing but a few dusty trunks, rotten floorboards and black widow spiders. I can tell by Jed's look that's exactly the place he wants to go.

Finally, there's the L-shaped pantry off Mrs. McDowell's kitchen with its big black coal stove that looks as if it should be good for cooking and baking treats for Pa. The pantry has one locked door and Mrs. McDowell keeps the key. "My kitchen is your kitchen to use as you wish," she says. "However, the pantry is my domain. If you need anything from it, check with me first."

Since Jed has no interest in pantries, he runs off to feed Samson and visit the chickens out back while Mrs. McDowell gives me a pantry tour.

I notice right off that she carries staples such as flour and sugar. What interests me particularly is a small jug of molasses that she has, one quarter full. Molasses is a key ingredient in shoofly pie. Pa does love his shoofly pie.

I want to bake that pie for Pa today! But I don't have the ingredients. I ask Mrs. McDowell if I may borrow hers.

"You don't feed a sick man pie," she says.

"You do when he's almost starved to death!" I find myself almost shouting the words. "My pa's so starved, he doesn't recognize his own kin!" I bite my lip to keep from crying the way that I did yesterday. I notice Mrs. McDowell is biting her lip, too.

"I suppose a little pie wouldn't hurt," she finally says. "But if you use my staples, I cannot replace them. Your fine General Milroy has forbidden all stores in Winchester from dealing with me unless I take an oath of allegiance to the Union. I refuse to do that."

"Can't Private Hardin get those staples for you?"

"Him? He's useless."

"Well if he can't or won't, I will. I'll replace any staples I use. I have a sutler friend . . . Mister Eli. He sells all kinds of things—molasses, sugar, mustache combs, dresses, hoops, *shoes*—"

"Shoes? Mercy me, this does sound promising." For

the first time all morning she's smiling. She says, "You know, my son and two of his boys have gone barefoot all winter. They do need shoes."

"Mrs. McDowell." I am so pleased I can help her the way she's about to help me, I am smiling, too. "Mister Eli will sell me all the shoes you need."

TWENTY

Shoofly pie, which has nothing to do with shoes except for the sound of the name, is not really a pie at all. It's a delicious molasses cake with a buttery piecrust below and a crumb-covered top. Some people prefer their shooflies dry on the bottom. Others prefer theirs gummy. My pa says, "The gummier the better."

Here is the recipe for gummy shoofly pie—enough to make three, which is the amount I always make, and it lasts my family at least three days, unless Pa is exceptionally hungry. Then it lasts two.

Line three deep pie tins with a rich pastry dough made with flour, butter and lard. Then, make crumbs out of 3 3/4 cups of flour mixed with 1 cup brown sugar, and 1 scant cup butter and lard. In a separate bowl, mix 1 cup dark molasses with 1 cup of hot water and a teaspoonful of baking soda. Pour the molasses mixture evenly into the three pie tins lined with pastry and then add your crumbs. Bake in a moderate oven for a half an hour, maybe longer.

The smell of shoofly pies fresh from the oven can, on a summer's day in New Oxford, draw flies from as far away as Gettysburg. Here on this rainy afternoon at Faraway it draws Joshua and Eggs 'n Bacon into the kitchen, which I have had to myself since Mrs. McDowell has gone to a prayer meeting somewhere outside Winchester and Jed's with Samson and the chickens. I haven't seen Joshua since last night. Where has he been? Has he been with pigs? I smell pigs.

"It's raining cats and dogs out there," he says as he takes off his rubber poncho.

"And why have you been out there in all that rain?" I ask.

"I helped Jed feed and groom your horse." He is talking to me as if I'm one of the boys.

"Since early morning?"

"No, I had other chores to attend as well," he says rather too easily. I think he's been up to something he doesn't want me to know about. I hope he's not a spy. "That Samson's a handsome horse," he blurts out. "Trumpeters ride horses colored gray like him. You didn't know that, did you? When officers need a call blown, they can spot their trumpeters if they're mounted on a big gray horse like Samson. The outcome of a battle can depend on a trumpet call being given at the right time.

"Bet you didn't know that, neither."

"No I didn't." Joshua sounds excited about trumpet calls and Samson. He'd better not try to steal Samson the way that Roscoe and Mister Eli did! "But I can tell you one thing, Joshua. Samson is a Bible horse and it would take more singing and praying than you know how to get him to step one foot onto a battlefield. So don't you even try!" I cut a piece of warm pie for Pa and slip it on a tin plate.

"I plan to be a trumpeter for Stonewall Jackson one day," Joshua says.

"Who's Stonewall Jackson?" I ask.

"Only the greatest general in the Confederacy!" He sniffs at the pie I've cut for Pa. The nerve of Joshua— talking about a Confederate general while sniffing a good Yankee pie! I move it out of reach.

He says, "Never in my born days have I seen a boy bake pie!"

I lower my voice. "Well, you haven't lived very long." I carry the piece of pie and a cup of boneset tea into the parlor. If these things don't wake up Pa, I don't know what will. Joshua and Eggs 'n Bacon tail me. I am walking barefoot now and without Cousin Ezekiel's brogans on, my bare feet pad as surely and quietly across the floor as Joshua's.

"Pa?" I kneel in front of him and hold the pie at his nose-level. He opens dazed-looking eyes. "I made you shoofly pie, Pa." He struggles to sit up; I have not seen him try to sit up since I arrived here yesterday! My hands are full and so Joshua steps in to help Pa, which I find surprisingly kind for a follower of Stonewall Jackson.

Sitting next to Pa, Joshua supports him the way I did this morning so that Mrs. McDowell could spoon-feed Pa his medications. Eggs 'n Bacon sits quietly against Pa's good leg and rests her nose in his lap.

Pa still doesn't look at me, but he looks at the shoofly pie I offer him. He takes a bite of pie, chews it slowly and then sighs. He takes a second bite and sighs. Without saying a word, he slowly eats and sighs his way through one whole piece of pie while I keep my growing excitement at bay—Pa's eating. Even though he doesn't know me, he's eating. I talk to him calmly about the little things of home: the swallows have returned; Anarchy got into a tussle with a skunk a few weeks back. And imagine this! Cousin Ezekiel has gone and bred our Lauden Honor to Miss Bemis's pet pig, Charity!

As I am saying this, I glance at Joshua. His blue eyes are glittering at me like the crystals in a geode. *Oh.* Pa clears his throat. I turn to Pa. He looks hard at me. In a voice I have not heard since he left home in December, Pa says, "Mein Gott, Anna Sunday. You do know how to bake a pie." And then, he slumps against Joshua. Pa has fainted! Never in my born days have I seen my pa faint! With Joshua's help, I sit Pa upright. I lightly tap his cheeks. He doesn't respond!

"What do we do now?" I ask Joshua.

"He looks all right," Joshua says. "His breathing seems deep and even. I think we should let him sleep."

Joshua helps me lay Pa down carefully on his side. I know that's the way he likes to rest with his head propped on a plumped-up pillow. "He'll be all right," Joshua says. I cover Pa in his soft blanket. Joshua tucks the blanket edge underneath Pa's clean-shaven chin. I have never known a boy to be so gentle.

We stay with Pa a little while, to make certain he's all right. On the way back to the kitchen, I fight to hold back my tears—*If I've done anything to hurt Pa . . .* Joshua says, "I don't think eating pie has harmed your pa." He holds open the kitchen door for me. "Eating a good pie always puts a man to sleep. It does that to me every time. When your pa wakes up, he'll feel stronger than before."

"I hope you're right."

"Of course I'm right. I'm always right. I was right the moment I first saw you. I knew there was something peculiar about you, Anna Sunday. You're a girl."

"Well, of course I am. But I am Adam to you and everyone else here except my pa, so help me God!" At the kitchen table, I sit down and put my head in my hands. At least Pa recognized me. At least he knows I'm here.

"I'll keep your disguise a secret; I'm good at keeping secrets." Joshua sits beside me. I smell pigs. A longing for home, for Cousin Ezekiel and Lauden Honor sweeps over me. The edge of Joshua's bare right foot comes to rest against the edge of my bare left one. Does Joshua realize his foot is touching mine? I don't move my foot; he doesn't move his. He says, "Do you like wearing trousers?"

"Would you like to wear skirts?"

"No. But I'd disguise myself in them if I had to. I'd wear them silly hoops and a frilly bonnet, too. I'd do most anything to be with my daddy."

"Your daddy?" I've been so caught up in Pa I haven't given any thought to Joshua's having a daddy or anyone else, except for his grandmother. "Where is your daddy?"

"He's with my two brothers; they're somewhere south of here—marching with Stonewall Jackson."

"I see." Are these the same men Mrs. McDowell wants me to order shoes for from Mister Eli? Are her barefoot kin Rebel soldiers marching with Stonewall Jackson?

Shoes make a soldier, Mister Eli said. Rebel soldiers, too.

I move my foot away from Joshua's and get up from the kitchen table. Oh why must everything be so complicated? Why can't everybody just have the good sense to stop fighting, go home, raise pigs and . . . and go barefoot same as Joshua and me?

TWENTY ONE

EVERY OCTOBER WHEN the maple leaves turn red, my ma's half-brother, Sam Falling-Water, comes down our road with his pack full of remedies to pay us a visit. Uncle Sam is part Delaware Indian and he knows the healing properties of plants. He brought us the very same Live-forever I now steep in medicinal water Joshua brought me from a spring out back. I am making a poultice to place on Pa's incision to draw out the infection. I've got to do something for Pa. He's been in a deep coma ever since he ate my pie.

While I baked and fed Pa that pie, Jed, the little soldier and now a self-made Yankee spy, has been ferreting out information. Not only from Joshua, who helped Jed groom Samson, but also from Private Hardin, who gave Jed our pa's ration of food for the week—a block of dessicated vegetables. I steep Live-forever and Jed tells me about his discoveries while forking apart the hard dry block of vegetables he's set in a pot of water to soak. Jed, who's never been interested in cooking, wants to make vegetable soup for Pa. I haven't had the heart to tell Jed dessicated vegetable soup is liable to make Pa want to stay in a coma forever.

"I found out how *Stonewall* Jackson, the Confederate general, got his name." Jed peels off a layer of moldy cabbage leaves from his vegetable block. "It was at the Battle of First Manassas. Yankee troops were everywhere and the Rebels were about to lose for sure. Still, Jackson held his line firm. General Bee, seeing this great show of courage and trying to rally Southern troops, shouted 'Look over there! There stands Jackson like a *stone wall!*'

"Know what I told Joshua when he told me this?" Jed holds up a forkful of what seems to be a dessicated turnip. "I told him, 'Before my pa went off to see the elephant and got shot, he made bricks. You can make an even stronger wall out of bricks.'

"I told that Joshua, 'Us Yankees are all strong bricks!' And do you know what Private Hardin told me? He said us Yanks must stand strong against the McDowells! He doesn't trust them, Adam. He says whenever he sees Joshua, Private Hardin smells trouble."

"Whenever I see Joshua, I smell pigs."

"And what do I smell cooking?" Mrs. McDowell says. The kitchen door has swung open and in she sweeps with her wet cloak still on from going to prayer meeting.

"Jed's dessicated vegetables and my steeping Live-forever." I hope she doesn't mind us taking over her kitchen.

"Live-forever?" She leans over my pot, cups the steam and breathes it in. When she lifts her head, her cheeks are red and she almost looks pretty. "Long ago, an Indian woman traveling through the Missouri town where I grew up gave my mother a poultice of this Live-forever to place on my injured hand. I'd stabbed it on a thorn and my palm had swollen twice its size.

"The poultice drew out my infection when nothing else could." Mrs. McDowell smiles at the memory. Then her expression grows more somber. "The woman was one of hundreds of displaced Potawatomi Indians on a forced march through our countryside. They had such courage. They kept placing one foot in front of the other—day after day—walking west toward a land they didn't want to go to and had never seen.

"Dear God," she says more to herself than to Jed and me, "I hope Mrs. Logan and her daughters have found courage to do the same."

"Who are the Logans?" Jed asks. I'm glad he's interested in Mrs. McDowell's story. I want him to like her.

"A fine Winchester family. That fiend General Milroy had them evicted from their home so that his wife could live there." Mrs. McDowell's cheeks flame bright red now. "He put Mrs. Logan and her daughters in a crude wagon, had them driven six miles outside of Winchester and then, he set them down by the roadside, completely destitute and we haven't heard from them since. It's been close to a month!"

With a slotted spoon, Mrs. McDowell lifts out a brown wet mass of my steamed Live-forever and inspects it closely. Will she yell at Jed and me for taking over her Rebel kitchen? Sometimes she scares me; I can't figure her out.

She glances sideways at me. "Tell me, Adam." She always calls me Adam. "How did you come upon this herb? I think we should use it on your pa."

Ever since he ate pie in the early afternoon, Pa's been asleep. Now it's after dark and he still won't wake up. Not when Mrs. McDowell and I try to give him his medications. Not when we apply Live-forever to his infected incision. I tell myself this is Pa's way of gathering strength. Once he's gathered enough, he'll break out of his coma. When he does, he won't just eat pie, say two sentences and faint. He'll talk, eat and act just like he did before he went off to see the elephant!

"Sleep is tired nature's sweet restorer." Mrs. McDowell smoothes Pa's reddish-brown curls away from his forehead.

"Can I read to Pa?" Jed wants to do something so Pa will realize his one and only son is at Faraway. I know.

"Read softly," Mrs. McDowell says.

Jed sits next to Pa and softly reads to him a poem Jed found in the *1863 Farmer's Almanac* that we brought with us from New Oxford:

Never Give Up!

Never give up! Though the grapeshot may rattle,
Or the full thunder-cloud over you burst;
Stand like a rock, and the storm and the battle
Little shall harm you, though doing their worst.

Never give up! If adversity presses,
Providence wisely has mingled the cup;

And the best counsel in all our distresses
Is the stout watchword of "Never give up!"

Jed stands up for that last line and shouts it by heart.
Afterward, Mrs. McDowell praises Jed for reading such
big words as *adversity* and *providence,* even though he did
yell that last line. Jed blushes. She says in a soft voice,
"You read well and with such expression! I'm sure your
father, even in his deep sleep, has heard you and is ex-
ceedingly proud."

Later, after Mrs. McDowell has left, Jed says to me,
"If Pa's so proud, why didn't he wake up and say my
name the way he did yours after you fed him pie?

"Pa won't ever give up, will he, Adam?"

"Did Mrs. McDowell's Potawatomi Indians give up?"
I say. "Did Stonewall Jackson?" This makes Jed perk up
his ears. "No! Of course not! And neither will our pa who,
being a brick, is so much stronger."

After this great show of courage on my part, the cold
wet night draws Private Hardin into the parlor to tend to
Pa's necessaries. The private stares sadly down at Pa and
tells us, "He's not long for this world."

This makes me so upset, my stomach cramps and I
throw up.

TWENTY TWO

THE GLOW FROM MRS. McDowell's lamplight seeps under the door to the study, where Jed and I are trying to settle down for our second night at Faraway. Private Hardin's off fixing supper for himself while Mrs. McDowell watches over our sleeping pa and writes letters on her rolltop desk. It's in a corner of the parlor not far from Jed and me. We can hear the scratching of her pen as we whisper back and forth. We don't know what she's writing now, but we do know what she wrote earlier.

It's only because Joshua, reaching up to snitch pie I'd placed on a high shelf, knocked over a bowl and it crashed to the floor. Mrs. McDowell ran into the kitchen to see what had fallen and Jed and I just happened to be near her desk. It's a fascinating desk—with a top that can be rolled up to reveal all sorts of little cubbyholes and secret drawers which, I'm certain, us Yankees living here are not allowed to open. Flat on the desk's writing surface for all to see was a letter she'd been writing:

My dearest Mary,

I have yet another opportunity to send you a letter care of our Joshua. I can't begin to tell you how helpful he has been. He is a clever and dear boy; he helps keep me in touch with those I love and yearn to see. And, with old Uncle Butler ill, Joshua has become Miss Adelaide's right hand. Joshua is a natural with pigs. But we've always known that, haven't we?

Yesterday brought two surprises, those two being Abraham Sunday's children. They're all of twelve and nine respectively and have traveled here from New Oxford, Pennsylvania, to be with their father. Imagine that! Such courage to travel so far during a time of war.

Mary, they know a sutler who might sell us shoes! Sometime over the next few days, I expect they'll speak to him about it. How it will relieve me when I finally know my son and grandsons are amply shod! It's a wicked world indeed, where soldiers must march barefoot.

I do believe our Abraham has taken a turn for the better since his children have arrived. His color has improved slightly. He is eating more. He sleeps a lot, but I believe it is a healing sleep. You know how relieved I will be if—no, I should say "when"—this dear man recovers. He is a good man, caught up in a tragic accident. But we've discussed this often enough. Suffice it to say, I am hopeful of his deliverance and

for mine as well. At prayer meeting today, I learned
that our beloved Stonewall has left his winter quar-
ters. The Yanks are fearful he might head this way,
which is music to my ears.

I hope that you are well and that my next missive
comes accompanied by shoes! Farewell my Darling.
Take good care of yourself & think of me with love as
I do you—

Mother McDowell

The contents of this letter keep Jed and me whispering, when we should be asleep gathering strength to get
Pa well before Stonewall Jackson comes. We discuss the
following:

1. Pa's health. Mrs. McDowell thinks Pa's getting better. Pa's not dying! Tomorrow, I will offer Pa more
shoofly pie and boneset tea. I will rub Pa's head the way
he likes. Jed says he'll give Pa dessicated vegetable soup
and read him Bible stories, including the one of how
Lazarus was raised after he was already dead.

2. Stonewall Jackson. Jed says, "Joshua told me
Stonewall loves Winchester. Stonewall plans to win it
back for the Rebs! And now, Mrs. McDowell's letter says
he's left winter quarters! Adam, we must get Pa better,
soon!"

3. Joshua McDowell. He was gone this morning because he helps Miss Adelaide care for pigs (I knew I
smelled pigs on him!). This is kind of Joshua. However,
he also *provides opportunities* for Mrs. McDowell to keep
in touch with those she loves through letters. Jed thinks
these letters contain a code which, when broken, gives

out key information on our Union troops. Jed says Mrs. McDowell and Joshua are spies. I don't agree. Jed says, "Then you spy on them, too. You'll see."

4. Spying. Feeling the burden of being Jed's older sister, I explain to him, spying is dangerous.

He says, "In war, it's necessary."

"It's not something you should do on your own," I say. "You could get hurt." Surprisingly, Jed agrees. He says, "We will spy together."

We seal our spying agreement with the Holy Bible Pact because I know it's the one sure way to keep Jed in line. Jed says, "Together forever!

"And while we have the Bible here, we must both swear not to buy shoes for Mrs. McDowell's Rebel kin!" He forces my hand down on the Bible even though I have not agreed to this oath! I throw Jed's hand off mine. "Of course I won't buy shoes for them!" I hiss. "But you shouldn't force me into swearing it. I hate to be forced into doing anything. I might get angry. What will happen if I get angry at you and I break the oath?"

"You'll bring on the end of the world with plagues of toads and ugly June bugs," Jed says.

Early the next morning, a bright sun casts a beam of light across the parlor floor and onto the carpet, green striped with big red roses on it. This is the first sunlight I've seen since we arrived at Faraway two days ago and it is a welcome sight. While I let Pa sleep a little longer before trying to give him shoofly pie and boneset tea, I sit in sunlight on a broad green stripe. I brush my short hair furiously and count the number of roses in the carpet. There are nine. According to Cousin Ezekiel, nine's a strong number; it's a sure sign of happiness and good things to come. This is because nine's a multiple of three—as in Father, Son and Holy Ghost.

Something suddenly blocks my sunlight and, for a moment, the parlor dims. I glance out the window. It's that old sourpuss, and Jed's *friend,* Private Hardin. He trudges across the front yard and disappears around the side of the house. He's headed for the servants' cabin where he plans to catch some shut-eye. He had to keep himself awake most of the night to make sure Pa wasn't dying on him. Pa was too darned quiet, Private Hardin said.

"Not one healthy moan out of him! Not one!" Private Hardin had a mournful expression on his face I wanted to scrub off with lye soap.

Well, I happened to be with Pa most of the night, too. I couldn't bear to leave his side. And although Pa's stillness worried me (Pa's face stayed so calm and still—nothing even twitched), I told Private Hardin, "Pa's is a healthy sleep! When he wakes up, he's going to be his old self; stronger than ever!"

"That's hogwash," Private Hardin said.

"It is not! Mrs. McDowell says Pa's color has improved. Mrs. McDowell says he's taken a turn for the better." I didn't say I read this in yesterday's letter meant for *dearest Mary.*

"And you believe the word of a Rebel she-devil over mine—a soldier in the Union Army?" Private Hardin said.

"I do when it comes to Pa."

"Then you're an addlepated idiot." Private Hardin went on to say Mrs. McDowell has kin in the Rebel Army! Well, I could have told him that myself! He said she couldn't be trusted. For all we know, she could be the one who shot my pa! That was the most ridiculous thing I'd ever heard! Private Hardin said, "Don't believe a word that she-devil says. Her word isn't worth a fart in a whirl-wind."

"Well, I happen to think it's worth a great big fart!" I said. Now, as I brush my hair on a good luck carpet with nine roses in it, I hear Joshua's trumpet playing "The Bonnie Blue Flag" to taunt Union pickets that are sup-posed to be stationed over some far ridge—*dump, da-dump, da-da-da.* I can't help but like this Rebel tune. It's far more cheerful than the gloomy words of a certain grumpy Union private who took care of Pa throughout the night. If Joshua's kin weren't marching with Stonewall Jackson, I just might buy those shoes for them.

TWENTY THREE

PRIVATE HARDIN'S NOT only a sourpuss, but he's an addlepated sourpuss! It's early afternoon on this first day of May. The sun that had shone earlier continues to shine and Dr. Beck, the surgeon in charge of Pa's care, has stopped by to check on him. Dr. Beck says in front of Jed, Mrs. McDowell and me that, in spite of Pa's still being groggy and unable to speak, his condition has taken a turn for the better. His fever is gone. Well, hallelujah! I wish Private Hardin were awake to hear this!

"He continues to be quite feeble," Dr. Beck says as he peers into my pa's eyes. "But his color has improved. His pulse is strong. I would hope that with continued care, he'd triumph over this pyemic infection, which earlier had suggested the gravest prognosis."

He attributes Pa's improvement to the "energetic regime of brandy, quinine, sesquichloroid and beef tea" the doctor recommended for him. As Dr. Beck is saying this, Pa raises his head and gives me a bleary-eyed stare.

I don't think my pa believes Dr. Beck. Pa's third eye—that funny bump between his eyebrows—is twitching. It's almost as if Pa's winking at me. My heartbeat quickens. Is Pa about to wake up?

After the doctor leaves, Pa awakens enough to eat a second piece of pie, a taste of Jed's dessicated vegetable soup and a cup of boneset tea! He takes a long afternoon nap and then, he sits up by himself. His mouth looks dry and so Jed runs off to fetch him drinking water from the medicinal spring out back. I gently wash Pa's face—his proud German nose, his hollowed cheeks, his third eye. "Look. Your beard's starting to grow in, Pa." His beard appears to be coming in gray. *Oh Pa.* "You're growing stronger by the minute," I tell him.

Pa looks me in the eyes and softly says, "It is not my beard that makes me strong. And it is not the doctor's medicine. *Das ist shlecht!* It is shoofly pie." Pa says this so naturally—as if we've been talking together all this time! I look closely at his eyes. They aren't bleary now. My pa's eyes are a sharp sky blue!

"Only my Anna could bake a shoofly pie this good," he continues slowly. ". . . Did my Anna travel here?" He wrinkles his brow and looks around. "But no. This is an impossibility."

"I'm here, Pa. Your Anna is here." He must not recognize me in my boy's disguise!

"I see this boy feeding pie to me." Pa goes on as if I hadn't spoken. "He has my Anna's sweet dark eyes and her round face with high cheekbones. This boy *is* Anna." Tears brim in Pa's eyes.

"Oh Pa!" I throw my arms around him and I hug him, but not too hard. "You're back! You're really back!"

"Pa's back?" Jed shouts from the front hall. Jed drops his pail of water and runs over to us as Pa says, "Why is my Anna wearing . . . dungarees? Why has she cut her hair?"

"She did it so that she could come to Winchester with me," Jed gasps. He kneels beside me all wet and muddy. "Cousin Ezekiel and I knew she'd be safer traveling this way, Pa. She's called Adam now. She vowed on the Holy Bible to stay Adam until she gets you home. That's what she says."

"She does this for me?" Pa frowns as he takes my hand in his. He places his other hand on Jed's shoulder.

"It's all right, Pa." I rest my cheek against his hand. "I'm used to dungarees. In fact, I like wearing them."

Pa says, "My dear children. You must go. Go now. Fetch your Cousin Ezekiel for me. Tell our good cousin, I want . . . I want him. . . . He must take you home."

"But Pa, Cousin Ezekiel can't take us home! He's not here!" I say.

"Not here? How can this be? I heard him in my head! He told me, 'Abraham, you are going to be raised up like Lazarus. A feast will be set out for you—rival soup, fried noodles, pork roast, shoofly pie.' "

"Now Pa, I know this sounds impossible, but I think you heard Cousin Ezekiel talking to you in his prayers!" I say. Oh this is a happy miracle! "I think you heard prayers coming all the way from New Oxford, Pennsylvania!"

"That's right!" Jed says. "You know how loudly Cousin Ezekiel can pray! Surely, he's been praying for you each and every minute we've been gone. He wants to keep you safe from Rebels."

"You'll have that feast he prayed for," I tell Pa while shooting Jed a nasty look. How dare he worry Pa with talk of Rebels! "Jed and I will make it for you." I don't know where we'll get the food for such a feast. From that old sourpuss, Private Hardin? From Mrs. McDowell? We'd have to pay her back. With shoes? I don't care.

"How did you and Jed find your way to me?" Pa says.

"Well," I say, "it started with 'Thumbelina.' "

"And the map you left," Jed says.

"Ay, yi, yi!" Pa says when we're done with a shortened version of everything that happened since we left home. We don't want to wear Pa out. "This is all too much for my befuddled head." He carefully lies down on his side. He bends his injured leg and I help him prop a small pillow beneath his thigh. He closes his eyes. "I must rest, eat and grow strong so that I can protect my children. And Ezekiel! He is living on his own! Mein Gott!" my dear pa whispers to his pillow. "What am I to do? I cannot believe my two young cabbage heads came all the way here alone."

TWENTY FOUR

I scour Faraway for food to strengthen Pa. I wrangle hardtack, beans and coffee out of Private Hardin. I gather eggs, dandelion greens and wild garlic to eat. I borrow staples, which I promise to replace, from Mrs. McDowell. I plead with Joshua to bring me a pheasant to roast. When he does, he teases me, saying I have to pay him back by making him an apple dumpling ("Your pa tells me you're his apple dumpling queen," that Joshua says). I stew four pig's feet Miss Adelaide sends for Pa in care of Joshua and with a note: *Thank you for trying to catch my pig. I hope you get well soon.*

"Eat and sleep. Eat and sleep. It's all that I have strength to do," Pa says to me now. It's been three days since he awoke from his coma and he hasn't even had the strength to try and walk yet. He has to walk if we're ever to leave here.

"You'll grow strong soon enough." I am rubbing Pa's head, which he dearly loves. Nearby, Jed reads aloud to us the Bible story of David who, with his slingshot, killed that giant Goliath by shooting him in the forehead with a stone. Jed pauses in his reading to ask our pa, "Do you ever wonder who shot you?"

Beneath my fingers, Pa gives a sharp intake of breath. Jed shouldn't ask such questions! Pa's too sick! He says, "It was a stray bullet, Jed."

"How do you know?" my rutchety brother says.

"It was an accident, Jed!" I speak before Pa can. I know Jed's been talking to Private Hardin. He told Jed the same thing he told me—that silliness about Mrs. McDowell! Pa likes Mrs. McDowell. Before he fell into a coma, she sat by his side and they talked together for hours. Like old friends, Pa said.

"Anna's right. It was an accident." Pa's the only one here who can call me Anna. "A hunter's stray bullet shot me. These hills are full of hunters—as I told you last night."

"These hills are full of Rebels," Jed says.

"I do not like to dwell on it, Jed," Pa says. "To do so is to go backward and grow downward, like a cow's tail."

"You don't want to be a cow's tail, now do you, Jed?" We should forget about Pa's being shot and move on. It's less scary that way. "Jed, why don't you fetch that paint box we brought for Pa?"

Jed scowls. Jed slams Cousin Ezekiel's Bible against the table. Jed kicks at a chair. But he does retrieve the paint box. Pa smiles softly as he runs his hand over the initials carved in the top of the wooden box—A.S., same as mine.

"You love to paint," I tell Pa.

"I must picture myself strong enough to paint." Pa opens the wooden box and fingers his handmade brushes.

"Once you're strong enough to paint, you can picture yourself strong enough to travel home." I smile to myself. It's the kind of thing Pa himself would say.

"This is true. But for now, I must sleep." He closes the box and hands it back to Jed. Smiling apologetically to me, Pa lies down on his cot and puts his folded hands beneath his head. "Sleep will strengthen my heart to paint. Painting will strengthen my soul for dreaming how to take my children home."

Oh I do love Pa. He says the nicest things. Unlike Jed. Jed's nothing but a rutchety cow's tail! Last night, Jed became so rutchety, he kicked apart our bedrolls! All because Pa and Mrs. McDowell told us we're not to step foot outside of Faraway. It's too dangerous. People don't know us. People could be out hunting. We could get shot.

"Joshua gets to go everywhere!" Jed stormed at me. "Joshua goes to Miss Adelaide's every morning. Joshua disappears for the rest of the day. I want to know what he's up to!"

"Well you can't." I was relieved we couldn't spy on Joshua. It's dangerous and besides I don't want to ever find out anything bad about him.

Why can't Jed be like Samson? Samson likes everyone here and they like him. Already the little one-eyed hen that Private Hardin once spat tobacco juice at has fallen in love with our Yankee plow horse. She nests in his manger. When we take Samson out to graze, the little hen follows with her head cocked so she can keep her eye on him.

Every so often, Samson will look back just to make sure she's there. Because of her one eye, I call her "Pete."

Joshua has fallen in love with Samson, too. Joshua feeds Samson for us every morning before heading out to Miss Adelaide's. It's early morning the day after Jed acted like a cow's tail and I visit with Samson and Pete. It's May fifth. Jed and I have been at Faraway for close to a week. I scratch Miss Pete's head and grumble to Samson about Jed, and who should come hobbling into the barn? The very Rebel Jed wants to spy on!

"You'll never guess what I did to myself this morning getting out of bed," Joshua says as Samson nickers good morning to him. "I twisted my ankle. Miss Adelaide lives a far piece away. It'd sure be nice if you'd let me borrow Samson, then I could ride him there."

"You can ride him." I feel a certain satisfaction at saying this. Riding Samson is something Joshua will never do. I straighten Samson's forelock so that it falls neatly between his ears. "All you need to learn is some Bible commands to make him go, stop and turn. And, of course, a certain Yankee hymn."

"Why would you want me to learn a dirty old Yankee hymn?" Joshua pets Samson's nose.

"Because if Samson becomes frightened or surprised by something, it's this hymn that brings him the courage to face it and keep on going. Right Samson?" I lightly rub his itchy spot. He wiggles his nose. I rub a little harder and Samson blows out his nose at Joshua. This startles Miss Pete off her nest and onto my head.

"If you don't sing the hymn, Samson will lie down on you. He won't budge until kingdom come," I say with a little brown chicken on my head. I gently remove her and tuck her underneath my arm. "And oh, you must sing the hymn loudly, because Samson's hard of hearing."

"What hymn is it?" Joshua asks.

I smile. "You have to guess."

"I'm not guessing at any Yankee hymn. And I tell you, it'll be a cold day in hell before I ever sing one," Joshua says, which I don't think is very nice—seeing as how I have to listen to his playing "The Bonnie Blue Flag" each and every morning.

The day on which Joshua refuses to guess at Samson's favorite hymn turns cold and fretful by afternoon. The sky blackens and we have a terrible storm with hard rain, wind, thunder and lightning. Joshua gets caught outside in it, which I believe he deserves for talking the way he did—swearing not only in front of me, but in front of a Bible horse and his friend, Pete.

Joshua, with Eggs 'n Bacon right behind, bursts into the kitchen where I am making soup. I see that Joshua's ankle has mended; he doesn't even limp. Eggs 'n Bacon shakes her body, spraying muddy water everywhere. Joshua's bare feet make wet splotches on the hardwood floor. I'm glad his grandmother is off at one of her prayer meetings. If she saw this, she'd have a conniption fit.

"What's that you're fixing?" Joshua asks.

"Rival soup for Pa." I concentrate on the rivals I'm rolling between my palms. They're little noodles made from egg and some flour and salt that I borrowed from Mrs. McDowell.

"I never heard tell of rival soup," Joshua says.

"It's made from chicken broth, corn and little noodles." I dump the rivals I've rolled into the steaming pot. "It's from Pennsylvania. Just like blancmange is from Virginia." Mrs. McDowell served us blancmange last night. It's a sweet pudding made from boiled milk, cornstarch and sugar. Pa liked it.

"Blancmange isn't a Virginia dish." Joshua takes off his wet poncho and hangs it, dripping, on a kitchen chair. "It comes from France."

"Isn't that a coincidence. So does the dress that my sutler friend Mister Eli bought for Mrs. Milroy." As soon as I say the name Milroy, I realize my mistake. One shouldn't say the name of a Union general's wife inside a Rebel household. Especially when that general's troops occupy the Rebel's town.

"From what I hear, Mrs. Milroy's no longer in Winchester to wear that dress," Joshua says with a biggest toad in the pond lilt to his voice. He thinks he knows everything. "She's so scared of us Rebels, she hightailed it to Indiana."

"I knew that days ago." I stir Pa's soup. I mustn't let any noodles stick to the bottom of the pan and burn. Pa needs all the noodles he can get.

"A battle's been going on." Joshua comes over and sniffs Pa's soup.

"Just listen to it out there," I say. "I wonder who will win—the thunder? Or the lightning?"

"I'm not talking about the storm." Joshua's voice has grown serious. "I'm talking about a real battle between General Hooker's forces and our Army of Northern Virginia under the command of General Robert E. Lee."

"General Lee?" Alarmed, I look directly at Joshua.

This Lee was the one who invaded the North last fall—until we stopped him at Antietam. "Where are the armies fighting?"

"At Chancellorsville. Miss Adelaide heard tell that us Rebels are winning. Stonewall, along with my daddy and two brothers, is there, so I reckon we are."

"Is Chancellorsville far from here?" I ask.

"As a crow flies, I reckon it's about a hundred miles."

"But it's farther by road? With mountains and rivers and big cities between there and here?" I want it to be thousands of miles from Pa. A battle close by could put him—all of us—in danger.

"I reckon. But if I was you, I'd tend to your daddy. I'd get him well real fast and take him home," Joshua says. "Stonewall loves Winchester; he hates to see it under Yankee control. Chances are, once he beats back those Yanks at Chancellorsville, he'll be heading here."

TWENTY FIVE

<small>OVER THE NEXT FEW</small>
days, all it does is rain, rain, rain—will it ever stop? Early
on the fourth day of the downpour, Mrs. McDowell declares, rain or no rain, she's going to prayer group. She
wants to find out what's happened at Chancellorsville. I
want her to find out, too. Private Hardin has already
claimed it a Union victory. He read it in the *Baltimore
American Newspaper*. But then Joshua said, "That newspaper's full of hogwash! General Lee's forces trounced
General Hooker's! Lee's right-hand man, Stonewall Jackson, penetrated to the rear of the enemy and defeated him.
Miss Adelaide says so."

I am secretly hoping the battle is a washout, with no
victory for either side. How can it be otherwise when all
we've had is rain? I don't want Union or Rebel forces
marching up to Faraway to threaten the McDowells or us.
All I want is time to get Pa strong enough so that Jed and
I can take him home.

On this fourth day of rain, Pa announces he's had
enough of living in a nightshirt. It's time he put on

trousers. And so, before she leaves for prayer group, Mrs. McDowell helps me dress Pa in some clothes that once belonged to her late husband—a soft white cotton shirt and dark wool trousers with braces to hold them up because Pa's so thin.

"You look smart, Abraham." She straightens Pa's collar. She's good with Pa. She likes him in a mother-son sort of way. The way Pa smiles at her, I know he likes her, too. They're friends.

"Now that I am dressed, I feel like learning to walk again," Pa tells us both. "Anna," he says (I love how he calls me Anna except when Private Hardin is in hearing. I will always and forever be Pa's Anna), "fetch my crutches!"

Leaning on these crutches, Pa stands. Once he's steady on his one foot, he smiles at us. "Now everyone. Stand aside. I have pictured myself doing this and I do it on my own." Using his crutches, he slowly moves across the parlor. One step. Then another. Step-by-step. Pa's walking! Soon we *can* go home! I'm about to tell Pa this when his right crutch catches on the carpet edge. Instinctively, Pa tries to stop himself from falling by catching himself with the foot that isn't there! Pa falls so hard, the floor shakes.

"I keep thinking I still have that foot," Pa says. Mrs. McDowell and I help him to a shaky stand. "I can feel it. I can feel my toes."

"But you don't have those toes, Abraham," Mrs. McDowell says gently. "You must constantly remind yourself of that. Otherwise, you'll keep stepping out on a foot that isn't there and fall." She speaks with Pa so matter-of-factly about his missing foot. I guess this is because she's a grandmother and used to talking about sad and missing things.

"I have no right foot," Pa says.

"That's right." She has tears in her eyes.

"It must make you feel off-balance, not having that foot there," I venture to say.

"Ay, yi, yi!" Pa says. "All these years I've been walking on two strong feet and now I just have one."

From the parlor window, I watch Mrs. McDowell climb into a buggy that's arrived to take her to her prayer meeting in Winchester. As soon as the buggy pulls away, I want it to turn around and bring Mrs. McDowell back. I like having her calm presence with Pa and me. I hadn't realized how difficult it would be for Pa to learn to walk with just one foot.

Mrs. McDowell doesn't return until late in the afternoon. She enters the parlor with a soggy newspaper under her arm. Her black bonnet and cape drip rain. She stares at Pa, Jed and me and says nothing.

Pa says, "Katherine, what is wrong?"

"Wrong? Why nothing's wrong." Her voice sounds as if it's about to break. "The South has won at Chancellorsville. General Lee's forces have triumphed over General Hooker's. The papers are full of it."

"I see." Pa clears his throat. My stomach lurches with the news. Will General Lee's army head here? If Stonewall Jackson has anything to do with it, they will. Jed, beside me, slams his hands against his thighs.

Pa says, "And your son and grandsons? Are they all right?" That's just like Pa—worrying over someone's kin.

"All three are alive. But my two grandsons are on crutches—their bare feet torn to shreds. Thousands of men on both sides have been badly hurt, Abraham. Thousands have died." She removes her wet bonnet. Her hair, usually pulled severely back into a bun, has come undone. Her untidy gray hair makes her suddenly look so old and fragile. I want her to be strong. I like her strong.

"Our Stonewall has been badly wounded," she says. I grow still inside. Jed, beside me, is all ears. "Why he had to go out scouting at night, I'll never understand. In the darkness, some of his own men mistook him for the enemy and shot him in the arm . . . They had to amputate that arm." Mrs. McDowell's voice has gone all thin and high. "War is such a terrible thing. Shot full of tragic accidents." She sits down, pulling at her bonnet ribbons. *"Dear Lord, his own men shot him."*

"A tragic accident shot our pa," Jed says.

The parlor grows so still then. All I can hear is the slash of rain against the windows and Pa, clearing his throat. Why did Jed have to bring up *that* tragic accident? Mrs. McDowell takes a deep breath, lets it out and says, "You're right, Jed. And now, all we can do is put that behind us and get your pa well.

"Oh this is a foolish war. A terrible war—one tragic accident after another. I dislike bringing talk of war into this house, but war is a fact; we cannot ignore it. And now, if you'll excuse me. *War* has given me a headache. I need to take a nap."

The rainy day turns into a wet black night. In the parlor, Mrs. McDowell, recovered from her headache, sits at her rolltop desk and writes out a list of things she wants me to buy for her tomorrow at the Union camp. Earlier, Pa asked Private Hardin to escort me to the camp— provided the rain stops. Pa wants me to buy all the goods from Mister Eli that Mrs. McDowell might need. Pa said, "We will replace her flour, sugar and molasses and I want you to buy her a present from me. Three cans of sardines. She loves sardines."

Life, even in war, must go on.

While I am at the Union camp, Pa wants me to find out all I can about this war. Does anyone know what Lee might be up to next? Are we still safe at Faraway?

I feel safe in Mrs. McDowell's parlor. And cozy, too. Mrs. McDowell writes her list. I knit a sock for Pa who sits on his cot and reads the Bible. Joshua, with Eggs 'n Bacon curled against his back, lies on the floor in front of the fire. A pig stepped on Joshua's left foot today. He's got that bruised foot propped up on a pillow that I brought him earlier and he repaid me with a smile.

Jed's the only fly in the ointment. Grumpy Jed, beside me on the sofa, picks at the calluses on his feet and buzzes angrily. He wants to go to Winchester with me and Pa has said no. He needs Jed here.

"It's not fair," Jed buzzes in my ear. "I'm the one who knows about war. I should talk to Mister Eli. I need to find out—"

"Oh shush, Jed." He's giving me a headache. I can take care of these things just as well as he can!

As Jed continues buzzing—*I should go with you. We should go together. We vowed, Together forever!*—Mrs.

McDowell pulls out a lower desk drawer and starts to rummage through it. "Where's that extra bottle of ink I bought? I know I put it somewhere." She yanks the drawer out further. She yanks too hard, for the drawer tips and falls to the floor, scattering all its contents. She cries, "Oh mercy me!"

Jed, Joshua and I rush over to help retrieve her scattered papers. I gather letters from *your dearest Mary,* and from *your son, John.* I pick up a daguerreotype—a black and white picture—taken of three laughing men on her front porch.

"Why that there's a picture of Daddy," Joshua says over my shoulder. He points to a man with happy eyes and light hair lounging against a porch column. "And that there's my two brothers, Robert and James."

These men are Joshua's kin? The Rebel soldiers on crutches and bare feet torn to shreds? I say the first thing that comes to mind, "Why Joshua, they all have golden hair like yours."

Before I even have the chance to blush, Jed cries out, "Mrs. McDowell! Look what I found!" He hands her a silver pin with three tiny chains attached. From each chain, something dangles—a whistle, a fancy carved silver vial and a long thin silver tube.

"Mercy me!" Mrs. McDowell gives Jed a big hug. She says, "My chatelaine! Here I thought I'd lost it. Was it in my desk drawer all these weeks?

"My late husband gave me this." She pulls the cap off the silver tube. A tiny wand, which has a small circle at one end, is attached to the cap. "There's still liquid!"

Looking over at my pa, she says, "Abraham. Watch this."
She blows through the circle and tiny bubbles drift out
into the room!

Pa says, "Ach. Such tiny bubbles!"

Mrs. McDowell dips the wand into the tube, brings it
out and blows again. Using his crutches, Pa stands. He
catches a bubble in his outstretched hand. A bubble lands
on Pa's reddish-gray beard. Circling him, Mrs.
McDowell continues to blow bubbles. A bloody battle
has just been fought at Chancellorsville and this sharp-
eyed Rebel woman with the iron gray hair surrounds my
tall thin Yankee Pa with bubbles as if—as if she's trying to
protect him!

Why I'd do anything for her. Anything!

TWENTY SIX

THE SUN HAS COME OUT. After four days of rain, a bright sun cuts a cheerful path across the muddy yard and into the barn where Miss Pete and Joshua watch as I try to bridle Samson for our five-mile trip north to the Union camp. I tell myself I have nothing to fear on this trip. The area to the north of Faraway is still under Union control—Pa says.

Samson's full of himself. He's accepted the bit, but each time I try to pull the crown of the bridle over his ears, he lifts his head so high, I can't reach it. There's only one remedy for this silliness. I wish Joshua wasn't here to learn it.

"Love the Lord your God!" I shout at Samson.

He cocks his head. Samson might as well be saying—*Are you serious?* His expression makes me feel guilty—using the Lord's commandment to make a horse bow down so that I can bridle him. But others use the Lord's name for far worse. "Samson! Love the Lord your God!"

He sighs, nuzzles Miss Pete, nesting in his feed box, and sinks to his knees. I slip on his bridle and quickly buckle it. When I shout the passage from the Song of Solomon to raise Samson up, Miss Pete flutters onto the top of his head. Samson, with the one-eyed hen nestling between his ears, follows me out of the barn.

"There's more to bridling and riding Samson than reciting Bible verses," I tell Joshua, hobbling alongside me. "So don't even think you can snitch him and ride off to Miss Adelaide's some morning."

"Now why would I do that?" Joshua says.

"Because you're always hurting something on yourself that makes it hard for you to walk." I glance at Joshua's injured foot. It's still swollen from where a pig stepped on it.

"You going to sing to Samson this bright morning?" Joshua asks.

"Not for you to hear." If Joshua knew it was "The Battle Hymn of the Republic" that gave Samson courage, he just might put aside his Southern pride to say—"I'll sing it if I have to," and then go ahead and steal our horse!

"You got the money Grandmother gave you? You got that list she wrote down of things we need?" Joshua asks.

"I certainly do." At the top of that list, Mrs. McDowell wrote down she needed three pairs of men's shoes, two sized eight and one sized nine. Do I dare buy those shoes? They're for Rebels who might even now be marching north toward us. Although I do think it would be hard to march when you're on crutches. Harder still to put shoes on over your shredded feet. They'd have to heal first. And Mrs. McDowell has been so kind . . .

Jed would have a conniption fit! Where is Jed anyway? I haven't seen his pouting face all morning.

"You're a good turn, *Adam* Sunday." Joshua puts his hand on my shoulder and he leaves it there.

"Well so are you, Joshua, and your grandmother, too." I am about to tell him how much they mean to me—so much that I might even buy shoes for them—when that grump Private Hardin comes trotting up. He rides a fat-bellied pony he tries to halt by standing in the stirrups and hauling on the reins. Joshua steps away from me. Mouth wide open, the pony keeps on trotting. He trots past us and carries Private Hardin into the barn, where the private starts swearing at him.

"Why I declare, that fool Private Hardin has gone and commandeered Uncle Butler's pony, Buckshot!" Joshua laughs. "You're going to have an interesting journey." He gives me a leg up on Samson and hands me the empty pack I am to fill with needed staples. I remove a protesting Miss Pete from Samson's head and hand her to Joshua. Samson nickers to his little friend. "They sure do like each other." Joshua tucks a muttering Pete beneath one arm. "They make an odd couple—this old Southern hen and your Yankee plow horse." I wonder if Joshua also thinks we're an odd couple—a pig keeper from the South and a Yankee farm girl dressed as a boy?

Private Hardin and Buckshot make an odder couple than do any of us. Buckshot is short and stubby while Private Hardin has such long skinny legs, if his feet weren't in the stirrups, they'd drag on the ground. Buckshot has a wild mane, a short thick neck and an iron mouth. When he gets it into his head to go somewhere, there's no stopping him.

Because of this, our journey to Winchester is as interesting as Joshua said it would be. We travel hither and yon, depending on where Buckshot wants to go next. He visits two little barefoot girls playing on the front porch of an old farmhouse. He stops to nuzzle some Union pickets lounging against a tree. He carries Private Hardin into a field and takes a bite of winter wheat. Nearing the Union camp just outside of town, Buckshot stops dead to watch a group of solders play horseshoes in the front yard of a large brick house. Nearby, a washerwoman boils clothes in a copper kettle. Yankee uniforms, their brass buttons sparkling in the sun, hang out on a line to dry.

Buckshot snorts. Jutting out his head, he grabs the bit between his teeth and takes off toward these uniforms. I expect Samson to tag along; he has all morning. But something else has caught his interest. At first, I think it's the soldiers drilling in the field off to our left. But no. It's a wagon. A single brown horse pulls a covered wagon along the crest of a hill in back of the tramping men.

Samson lets out a whinny loud enough to praise the Lord from Winchester to New Oxford. I don't even have a moment to yell at Private Hardin—"That's Mister Eli's wagon!" because an excited Samson has grabbed the bit between his teeth. I grasp his mane as he tears off at a gallop to greet an old friend and fellow plow horse— Dixie.

Mister Eli sits in his green and red striped camp chair. He's positioned it just at the entrance to his sutler's tent so that we can keep a lookout for Private Hardin. It's been almost an hour since I last saw him heading toward that clothesline full of Yankee uniforms. I wonder if Private Hardin is all right?

Seeing as how I am "a distinguished ambassador for peace" (I like that Mister Eli calls me this; it sounds so important), Mister Eli has given me the honor of sitting in his newly acquired blue and gray striped camp chair. Mister Eli says I am an ambassador for peace because I have a fearless heart. I am unafraid, nay, *unabashedly unafraid,* to purchase goods from him for what he calls "the suffering denizens of both the North and South." I am unsure what he means by *denizens.* Does he mean soldiers? I have purchased nothing for any Southern soldiers; only Mrs. McDowell has. Her money has paid for the three pairs of men's shoes that Mister Eli doesn't have right now, but he'll order for the end of the month. I had nothing to do with it. I only handed Mister Eli the money and Mrs. McDowell's list.

"Is there anything else you or this Mrs. McDowell might need?" Mister Eli asks me now.

"No." I squirm a little in my dignitary's chair. Jed will kill me for what I did, even though I really didn't do it.

Mister Eli takes a cigar out of his vest pocket. He's wearing that silver dragon vest he wore the first time that I saw him. He lights his cigar and puffs on it until the end burns as red as a dragon's eye. He says, "How's your father?"

"Pa's mending slowly." I have refrained from asking Mister Eli my pa's question—are we safe at Faraway? I've been afraid to hear the answer. We're all content at Mrs. McDowell's. Well, at least most of us are. But I have to face things. So I ask Mister Eli about Robert E. Lee,

Stonewall Jackson and does Mister Eli think they'll march north to attack the Union forces at Winchester?

"From what I hear, no one in command seems to know what the Army of Northern Virginia will be up to next," Mister Eli says. "Particularly with so many badly injured soldiers, including Lee's right-hand man, Stonewall Jackson. However, as a sutler who trades with both sides, I've heard talk that brings me goose bumps even in my sleep." Mister Eli leans so close to me that I can see the dark hairs growing in his nose. He says in a lowered voice that gives *me* goose bumps, "Dear Adam. Keep your eyes wide open, your carpetbags packed and be ready to flee at a moment's notice. Winchester is a powder keg about to explode."

TWENTY SEVEN

PRIVATE HARDIN NEVER appears at Mister Eli's tent to escort me back to Faraway. I fear something terrible has happened to him, although Mister Eli says, "He's probably at some tavern trading war stories with his friends." I return to Faraway at dusk with my pack full of provisions (including Pa's gift of sardines for Mrs. McDowell). Jed awaits me in the barnyard. Jed pounces all over me with questions. "What happened to you? Why did you take so long? I thought Rebels had attacked you! Did you see Mister Eli? Where's Private Hardin?"

While I walk a sweated Samson to cool him off, I tell Jed everything that happened except for Mister Eli's dire prediction—*Winchester is a powder keg.* I haven't decided how to deal with that. How can we flee at a moment's notice when Pa can only walk from the parlor to the kitchen and back? I hope Dr. Beck comes by soon. He'll know how to get Pa stronger faster. I save the delicate matter of *shoes* for last.

"You said you wouldn't buy shoes! You swore it on the

Bible!" Jed says when I am done. He's so angry with me, he kicks at a pile of steaming horse manure.

"You made me swear it." I am trying to stay calm. "Besides, *I* didn't *buy* shoes. Mrs. McDowell *ordered* them."

"It's the same thing!" Jed says.

"No it's not!"

"Yes it is! You broke a Bible Pact! And now . . . And now the whole world's coming to an end." Angry tears fill Jed's eyes. What is wrong with him? He's making a tempest in a teapot! He says, "You should have taken me with you! You never should have left me on my own."

"Something happened here while I was gone," I say.

"No it didn't." Jed's face has turned bright red. He's lying.

"Did you do something you shouldn't have while I was gone?" I say. Then it comes to me. "Oh Jed! Did you spy on Joshua?"

"Now why would I do that?" Jed says with his bright red face. "Do you think I want to bring on the end of the world with thunder and lightning and plagues of ugly toads and June bugs by breaking a Holy Bible Pact the way you did?"

"What happened here?" I say.

"Nothing. Only Mrs. McDowell had a conniption fit because she saw me fiddling around at the edge of the woods. She said, 'You have no business being near the DANGEROUS BACKWOODS.' And here I was, just looking for crayfish in the little creek!

"She said, 'Look at this!' She swished her walking stick through the grass to show me a big rock about the size of my head. She said, 'This is where your pa hit his head after someone shot him. If there hadn't been snow and rain to wash it off, you'd still be able to see his blood.'

"Mrs. McDowell said she saw our pa get shot! She was in the garret! Through the high-up garret window, she saw our pa running through the woods. She heard a shot and he fell down. She told me she never wanted to see anything like that again. She said, 'If I should find you sprawled on the ground—shot through the chest or arm or leg—I don't know what I'd do. I will have no more Yankee blood on my hands,' she said. She was so angry, she scared me."

"She doesn't want to see you hurt." I'm glad that Mrs. McDowell scared Jed. Now, he'll stay put.

"She's an old toad," Jed says. "I don't like her."

"She was only trying to protect you."

"If she wanted to protect me, she'd go into those DANGEROUS BACKWOODS herself! She'd get rid of that Gray Man . . ." Jed stops.

"What Gray Man?" I don't like the sound of this.

"Oh nothing." Jed kicks apart a dried manure patty.

"Tell me, Jed!" I grab his arm and make him look at me.

"It's nothing," he repeats.

"Are you making up this Gray Man?" A few years back, Jed made up Mister Salt and Pepper. He came out after dark and told Jed if Pa didn't personally cover Jed's toes with his blanket, Mister Salt and Pepper would eat them.

"Maybe." With a reddened face, Jed kicks apart a second dried manure patty. "Adam, did Mister Eli say anything about the war?"

"He says no one knows what the Rebels are up to, but that we . . . we should stay on our guard." I'm not about to tell Jed, who's kicked apart a steaming pile of horse manure and now two dried manure patties, that Winchester is a powder keg.

In a small voice, Jed says, "Adam, when is Private Hardin coming back?"

The next day, through Dr. Beck, who's come to check on Pa, we learn that Private Hardin is never coming back! He can't! When Buckshot took off with him toward that clothesline filled with Yankee uniforms, the clothesline caught Private Hardin in the chest and flipped him over backward. He did a full back somersault and came down the wrong way. I say the wrong way because when Private Hardin landed, he broke his leg. Now he's convalescing in the hospital.

"I could assign another soldier to your care," Dr. Beck tells Pa.

"That will not be necessary," Pa says before I can interject that—"Having a Union soldier here might be a good idea." Pa doesn't know about the explosive state of Winchester, because I didn't tell him. And I made Jed promise not to worry Pa with his story about a Gray Man. If Pa worries, he won't eat. Pa needs to eat. He needs to grow strong so that he can walk. Even with Samson to carry him, Pa still needs to walk at times.

"Each day I grow a little stronger," Pa is telling Dr. Beck. "Yesterday, I walked from the parlor to the kitchen and back—three times! I do more things for myself. And I have my children. They take good care of me."

My dear pa. I can hardly believe he's getting so much stronger. But not strong enough.

"I won't be around anymore to check on you," Dr. Beck tells Pa. "Tomorrow, I leave for Chancellorsville. There are thousands of wounded to tend to there. You could move to the hospital in Winchester. You'd be safer there. Only, there's been an outbreak of typhoid fever. . . ."

"I will not have my children exposed to typhoid," Pa says to my great relief. I don't want him exposed to it, either. People with amputated limbs are susceptible to all sorts of things. Why at this very moment, Mrs. McDowell is at an emergency prayer meeting for Stonewall Jackson with his amputated arm. He's come down with pneumonia.

"It's isolated out here; I worry for your safety," Dr. Beck says. "No one knows where the Rebels will head next. Our pickets draw closer to town."

"We will manage," Pa says. "When do you think I will be well enough to travel home?"

"If you have no more setbacks and continue to make progress, I'd say in about six weeks," the doctor says.

"Six weeks?" Pa makes a face while Jed and I stare at each other in panic. Six weeks takes us to the end of June! Only God knows where the Rebel Army will be by then. To say nothing of Jed's Gray Man in the DANGEROUS BACKWOODS.

Last night, Jed prayed—"Dear God. Keep us safe from the Gray Man." Afterward, in bed, Jed told me that the Gray Man has burning eyes, the fingers of his right hand are melted together and he's all gray, from his long hair, to his ragged clothes, to his bare and bleeding feet.

TWENTY EIGHT

AFTER DR. BECK LEAVES, Pa says, "Anna! Jed! It is time for me to paint!" I cannot believe my ears! He *is* feeling stronger. He tells us Mrs. McDowell has an unfinished blanket chest in her garret that she says could use his artist's touch. Pa says, "Fetch that chest for me now!"

I'm afraid of the garret. It's one of those places Mrs. McDowell says Jed and I are not allowed. If only she was back from her prayer meeting! She could guide us around the rotten floorboards and black widow spiders. However, as Jed reminds me, "If Pa tells us to fetch a chest from the garret, then fetch it we must!"

The garret isn't as old and falling apart as Mrs. McDowell made it out to be. The floorboards look sound and the garret is filled with stacks of old feed bags, boxes, barrels, trunks, broken furniture and rolled up rugs tucked beneath the eaves. It reminds me of ours at home, only Mrs. McDowell's is neater. Still, I feel uneasy.

"Watch out for spiders!" I try to joke with Jed as he follows me between trunks and barrels toward a large unfinished chest that stands beneath a back window. The sun pours through this window. It's remarkably clean for a garret window. I lean over the blanket chest to peer out and notice a bottom square of windowpane is missing.

"Mrs. McDowell should fix this broken pane," I call to Jed. "Bats could get in." Through the window, I see the back field of Faraway that dips down to the stream where Jed was caught catching crayfish. Beyond it, rises a wooded ridge that is turning green with spring.

"It was through this window that Mrs. McDowell saw our pa get shot," Jed says in back of me. "She told me she never wants to see that sort of thing again. She wants no more Yankee blood on her hands, she said. 'You must never go near those DANGEROUS BACKWOODS,' she said."

"I know that. You already told me." I turn to Jed and my eye is caught by a small brass nameplate on the top of the blanket chest. The nameplate has the word *Katherine* inscribed in it. "This isn't any old blanket chest." I point out the nameplate to Jed. "It's Mrs. McDowell's special blanket chest, only someone never finished it for her. Pa will."

"Is the name Katherine the same as Kate?" Jed says.

"Kate could be a nickname for Katherine."

"Oh." From the stricken way Jed says this, I can tell that something's wrong. He glances sideways so he won't have to look at me—only at some broken drop-leaf table. He says, "Oh no. Oh no." When he turns back to me, his eyes have grown as large as those cow patties he kicked apart yesterday.

"What is it?" I ask.

He points to that broken table next to the blanket chest. The table's been propped up on its side, with the tabletop facing us. Out of the cubbyhole formed by the top and its two leaves protrudes something I had not noticed before—a long gun barrel with something attached. A telescope? Why it's a rifle with a telescope attached, the same as One-Eyed Pete's!

"A sharpshooter could hit a target over a thousand yards away with that," Jed says.

"What's it doing up here?" Instinctively I whisper.

"Being kept hidden in a secret place. Mrs. McDowell uses it to fight off us Yankees," Jed whispers back.

"She has a pistol for that."

"A pistol's only good up close." Jed's eyes fill with tears. "Adam, do you know what I think I know? I . . . I think Mrs. McDowell poked that telescopic rifle out that broken panel in her garret window and she . . . she shot our pa with it."

"Tomorrow, I will prepare the *Katherine* chest for painting," Pa tells Mrs. McDowell—back from her prayer meeting where she learned Stonewall Jackson is not doing well. "But for now, I will sit here and enjoy the sun." Jed and I carried the *Katherine* chest out to the back porch for Pa and he sits on a chair beside it. This is the first time he's come outside since *someone* shot him. I made Jed swear not to tell Pa who he *thinks that someone is.* Because it *isn't. It can't be.*

"See how the sun's rays light up the field?" Pa tells Mrs. McDowell. "Look at it, tumbling down to the little creek and those dark woods beyond."

Jed's Gray Man lives in those dark woods.

"That field is turning green with spring." Mrs. McDowell puts her hand on Pa's shoulder and he smiles up at her. For a moment, there's no talk of Stonewall Jackson, General Lee, Chancellorsville or soldiers with shredded feet. She says, "It's spring, Abraham. I do believe you love the spring." She gently squeezes Pa's shoulder. And then, her gaze travels from Pa, to her *Katherine* chest and over to me. She looks hard at me. I detect a probing question in her eyes—*When you were in my garret, did you see a gun?*

At night, in the study with all the rocks and geodes full of secrets and the light from the parlor fire seeping underneath our closed door, Jed whispers to me, "What are we going to do now? We have to do something! There's a Gray Man in the woods behind us and a telescopic rifle two floors above."

"We're going to sit tight and get Pa well. Besides, that rifle is broken." I have thought about this ever since Mrs. McDowell shot a certain look at me and this is what I have decided.

"What if it's not broken? What if she shot our pa with it?" Jed says.

"What if she did, Jed? What-if-she-did?" Hot tears flood my eyes. I have thought about this, too. "If she did, then I suppose one of us should just travel to the Union camp and tell General Milroy about it. And then, he'll send us to an orphan's home. He'll put Pa in a hospital that's full of typhoid fever. He'll transport Mrs. McDowell and Joshua south without food or clothing, the way he did that poor Logan family. General Milroy's soldiers will, no doubt, take over Faraway. As for Samson's little friend, Miss Pete? Those soldiers will eat her."

"I don't want to put Pa in the hospital." Jed throws himself into my arms and he starts sobbing. *Oh Jed.* I lean my cheek against the top of his head. He says, "I don't want to hurt Miss Pete."

"Then don't bring up the rifle!"

"Even if I have to lie to Pa about it?"

"Did you say something to Pa?"

"No." Jed wiggles himself close inside my arms. "He just noticed that I've been acting glum. He wanted to know why. I lied. I said I had a stomachache. I didn't tell him about the Gray Man, either."

"Well, under certain circumstances, I suppose it's all right to lie. Sometimes, I suppose, we have to lie—to protect ourselves and those we love." I've just done some lying—to Jed and to myself. I have told myself that Mrs. McDowell did not shoot Pa when my heart of hearts tells me that, through some sort of *tragic accident,* she did.

TWENTY NINE

AFTER SEVERAL DAYS of Pa's slow and careful work, the *Katherine* chest is ready for a base coat of milk paint. This paint is made from milk that's been skimmed, clotted and had a good large dash of lime added to it. After that, you add your pigment. I told Pa he should use the clay Jed and I brought from home. It would make the base coat a lovely New Oxford reddish-brown.

Jed disagreed. Jed told me the base coat should be black because that's the color of Mrs. McDowell's treacherous heart. To Pa, Jed said it should be black because it's Mrs. McDowell's favorite color. Doesn't she always dress in black? So now, with a small bowl of prepared milk divvied up among several sardine cans, Pa keeps Jed busy experimenting with different pigments Jed's found—dirt, decayed leaves, egg yolk, tree bark, chicken bones—to see if he can come up with an acceptable shade. "It must not be too dark or gloomy," Pa says.

Jed's look seems to say—*the gloomier the better*.

Now he's run off to gather lampblack from all the oil

lamps in the house. Meanwhile, Pa dozes in the warm spring sun. Joshua's off hunting partridges for supper. Mrs. McDowell is hanging Pa's sheets out on a line to dry, and I sit on a bushel basket in the barnyard, peeling winter apples for apple dumplings. Miss Adelaide sent these apples care of Joshua. Faraway seems like such a peaceful place. Except for Jed. Rutchety Jed with his black paint and his Gray Man stories.

"The Gray Man lives in a cave!" Jed says. "He gathers white stuff from a cave and loads it in a wagon marked CSA! That stands for the Confederate States of America!" Jed doesn't know what the white stuff is. But there are a number of science and rock books in Angus McDowell's study. "I mean to read them until I find the answer. I'm sure that white stuff is dangerous and has to do with war," Jed says.

Oh. Now would you look at that! Jed's caught up with war and meanwhile Miss Pete and Samson are playing *tug-of-war* with an apple peel! Samson, head lowered, pulls gently on one end of the peel. Miss Pete, neck outstretched, pulls furiously on the other. She's no match for a Yankee plow horse! But there's a kindness in Samson that allows Miss Pete to think she is.

Fluffing out her feathers, Miss Pete stops pulling and eyeballs Samson. Samson nickers. Miss Pete gives a good hard jerk. Samson lets go and there goes Miss Pete—splat on her rear end, but still holding on to the peel. In triumph, she waddles behind the manure pile to eat it.

"Here you go, Samson." As I throw him another peel, who should I hear whistling "The Bonnie Blue Flag"? Joshua! He strides up the back field with an old musket, a brace of partridges flung over his shoulder and Eggs 'n Bacon bounding alongside him. I often wonder where Joshua spends his days. But I don't want to hear his answer because I've made up my own. When he's not hunting, Joshua spends his days tending pigs.

Still whistling, Joshua starts to climb the barnyard wall. Now why doesn't he just walk around and enter the barnyard by the gate? That's what a sensible Yankee would do.

"Look what I shot!" Joshua clears the top of the wall. But then, as he hops down, the butt of his musket catches on a stone and upsets his balance. Joshua falls splat in the barnyard on his rear end—just the way that Miss Pete did! Ignoring the fact that Joshua's covered in dirt and bits of manure, I say, "It looks like you had a successful hunt."

"Your pa will have a feast tonight." Joshua smiles and I notice for the first time that he has freckles on his aquiline nose. It is, in spite of Joshua's being a Rebel, a princely nose. Do princes have freckles? He says, "Want to go down to the millpond and skip some stones with me?"

The millpond stands on the opposite side of the house from the backwoods. The little pond feels cozy in its hollow of land bordered by the mill, a gentle ridge and the big house at Faraway rising in the distance. I like it here.

"To skip rocks, first you find a good rock—slick, flat and circular and it feels good in your hand." Joshua holds up a rock he's found. He's teaching me to skip rocks because I've never done it. He says, "Then you throw it kind of parallel with the water and the rock becomes alive! It skips and skips and if you do it right, why that rock can skip forever." He skips a rock along the water and Eggs 'n Bacon leaps into the millpond after it. So, of course, the rock doesn't skip forever. But it does skip seven times.

"Now you try it." Joshua hands me the rock that Eggs 'n Bacon has retrieved. I do exactly as Joshua has said and the rock goes splat without skipping once.

"You're throwing like a girl," Joshua says.

I watch Joshua carefully and after several false starts, I get it right. My rock skips as many times as his. My rock has come alive! As I fling it again, Joshua tells me once the war is over, he plans to be a trumpet player in a traveling circus. And what do I plan to be?

Before I went off to see the elephant and learned to skip rocks, I would have answered immediately, "I want to be a wife and mother and keep a warm and happy house." I still might. But I can't tell Joshua that! Not while I'm in trousers! Watching Eggs 'n Bacon, bottoms-up in the millpond and searching for the rock I threw, I take a good long think. "Well, I can't play any instrument," I finally say. "I don't sing well. But I am good with my hands and I am kind. I could be a doctor or . . . or I could be what my friend Mister Eli calls—*an ambassador for peace.*"

"Really?" Joshua grins as Eggs 'n Bacon bounds up to him with a rock in her mouth. Joshua thinks I'm being funny. Well, I'm not. I think there's a real need in this world for peace ambassadors and it takes an extremely kind and forgiving heart to be one.

Eggs 'n Bacon nudges Joshua. She dumps the rock into his outstretched hand. It's not the flat stone we've been throwing all this time. It's round and shaped like an egg. Joshua says, "Well I declare. This must be one of grandfather's rocks that Eggs 'n Bacon stole and dumped in the millpond. Think it's a geode? Want to crack it open?"

"No!" I surprise myself by how strongly I feel about this. But some things should remain secret. Because, because it leaves us room to dream!

"Here. Take it, peace ambassador. It's yours." Joshua opens my hand. He places the rough-surfaced rock into the palm of my right hand. He cups that hand with his. Here I am, a Yankee girl with ugly chopped off hair and ears sticking out and a Rebel prince holds my hand. It tingles and I feel a peculiar warmth inside. I wonder if Samson feels this kind of warmth when Miss Pete perches between his ears?

THIRTY An apple dumpling

is a little like a geode—ordinary on the outside; inside it holds all its beauty which, in the case of the dumpling, happens to be an apple. To make an apple dumpling, you first place a peeled and cored apple in the center of a square of pie dough with the cored hole up. You fill the hole with white sugar mixed with a pinch of cinnamon. Top the sugar mix with a tablespoon of butter. Then lightly brush water on the four corners and outer edges of your pie dough square. Fold the corners up to the center to meet and pinch the corners and all seams together to seal. Brush with melted butter. Bake in a hot, but not too hot, oven until the apple is tender—about forty-five minutes or so—and then serve warm with cinnamon-sugar mixed with cream.

In times of war, apple dumplings like this can be costly to make, what with the price of sugar being so high and cinnamon hard to come by, especially in the South. For ours, I skimp on the sugar, since Miss Adelaide's apples taste sweet anyway. I use small pinches of

Mrs. McDowell's precious cinnamon and I only make six dumplings—two for Pa and one each for Jed, Joshua, Mrs. McDowell and me.

Since I am fixing such a *scrumptious dessert*, Mrs. McDowell cooks a feast to go along with it. For the first time since we've been at Faraway, we all feast together at Mrs. McDowell's dining-room table. Pa sits at the head with Mrs. McDowell facing him. Jed sits across from me. Joshua, beside me, says grace: "Bless this food oh Lord, and General Stonewall Jackson. May he come to renewed strength."

"Bless President Lincoln, General Hooker and our great Union Army," Jed says and I say quickly, "Dear God, bless them all, Reb and Yank alike, amen."

By candlelight, we eat roast partridge, watercress salad, bread and steamed corn pudding off Mrs. McDowell's China flowered plates while she and Pa discuss the *Katherine* chest. Mrs. McDowell would like Pa to decorate it with scenes of his Pennsylvania home. That way, she says, she can see through his eyes and hands the brick house and farm he speaks so lovingly about. Smiling at Mrs. McDowell, Pa says, "I have never decorated a chest this way, but to do so would bring me joy."

Mrs. McDowell goes on to say that a New Oxford reddish-brown should make the perfect base coat for the scenes. As for Jed's special black paint, she says, "It will do for outlines and borders."

Feeling mildly triumphant, I smile across the table at Jed. He flips his fork in the air as if to say—*so what if your color won!*

At dessert, Mrs. McDowell declares my apple

dumplings are the best she's ever had. Pa says, "Anna's dumplings are like life. You bite deeply and are surprised with the sweetness you find inside." My pa says the nicest things. Joshua says, "These sure are good apple dumplings," and his bare foot brushes against mine. Only Jed says nothing. But I notice he's eaten the dumpling I made. Every bite.

It's a happy night for me. For the night, I can almost forget a war is going on shot full of *tragic accidents*. But then, the next day, war news arrives at Faraway. Mrs. McDowell's prayer group brings it and the news is so upsetting, the three ladies burst out with it while congregating with Mrs. McDowell on her front porch.

Stonewall Jackson, the Savior of the South, has died.

"Who will stop the Yankees now?" a lady on the front porch wails. "Those wretched Yanks have destroyed our homes!" She shoots a nasty look at me—standing next to Joshua at the dogwood. "They've torn down our barns. They've stolen our milk cows. They've eaten our pigs and chickens. They've trampled all our lilac bushes. Who will stop them now? How can we go on without our Stonewall!"

"We will go on because we have to," Mrs. McDowell says in that firm way she has. "We will continue to place one foot in front of the other the way we always have. We *will* survive." She looks at Joshua while she speaks. He's been at the millpond with me. Our trousers are rolled up to our knees because we've been wading together in the water while skipping rocks. Joshua's face is as white as stone.

After learning of his hero's death, Joshua is gone from Faraway even more than before. He never plays his trumpet. Days go by where I hardly see him. He only seems to come to the house to eat, sleep and help his grandmother with chores. Jed says, "Joshua probably spends all his time with the Gray Man now."

"Joshua's probably with Miss Adelaide's pigs. Pigs can be a comfort when you're feeling sad." Our own pig Lauden Honor was. He'd let you hug him while you cried and cried. "There's one good thing about this, Jed. With the death of the Savior of the South, perhaps the War between the States will end."

"That won't ever happen," Jed says. "There's still General Lee." But Pa says, "Maybe Anna. We can hope."

Meanwhile, Pa covers the *Katherine* chest with scenes that make me homesick—our house with smoke curling from its chimney into our deep blue Pennsylvania sky; Cousin Ezekiel's garden full of blossoming tulips; Miss Bemis's pet pig, Charity, with six piglets nuzzling at her teats. As Pa paints, his leg slowly heals and he gains weight, growing stronger. Jed spends time on the back porch with him, reading books. Jed's still determined to find out about the white stuff in the Gray Man's wagon.

I continue to nurse Pa. I cook. I clean. I wash clothes. I skip rocks at the millpond. And then, on the last day of May, Joshua joins me at the millpond as if we've never been apart. He sits beside me on the bank and we cool our bare feet in the still dark water. Joshua's golden hair is matted and dirty and he has dark circles under his eyes. He still mourns his hero's death, I know. And so, I tell

Joshua what Pa says—hot fires make strong bricks. I say, "Joshua McDowell, you're a strong brick. You'll survive the death of Stonewall Jackson."

"Adam Sunday." Joshua always calls me Adam even though he knows that I'm a girl! "You are the kindest Yankee I have ever met. And do you know what I vow to you? Even though Grandmother and I have our own kin to tend to and worry over, still, we will always protect you and your family. I guarantee that with my life!"

I find this a surprising thing for Joshua to say. What is there to protect us from? The Rebels? But their savior has died. Joshua does another surprising thing. He runs off, but not before leaning over to kiss my cheek. I think he kissed my cheek. I am almost certain he kissed it. I felt something there—like the warm flicker of a butterfly's wings.

THIRTY ONE

In "Thumbelina," after the tiny girl saves the swallow's life, he flies away with her to a warm country where the air smells of fresh oranges. In the middle of this paradise, they come upon a palace surrounded by gardens of white flowers. The swallow sets Thumbelina down on the most dazzling flower of all. And who should pop out of that flower but the handsome prince with an aquiline nose! He is so pleased at seeing the beautiful Thumbelina! He places his crown on her head, asks her what her name is and would she become his wife and be queen over all the flowers.

"Why yes, of course," she says.

"Why yes, of course," I whisper. I am pitching manure into Mrs. McDowell's wheelbarrow, which I then will wheel over to her vegetable garden. There, she and Jed will work the manure into the bone dry soil to fertilize Mrs. McDowell's tomato plants. She is determined to place one foot in front of the other by growing the biggest tomatoes in the valley. This is in spite of the fact that we've had so little rain over the past few weeks, the plants themselves could die.

Alongside the old springhouse, white hedge roses are in bloom. As I push the now-filled wheelbarrow past them and over to the garden gate, I breathe in their sweet scent. In "Thumbelina," after she agrees to be queen, a lord or a lady pops out of each white flower she passes. They offer her lovely gifts. The prince offers her the loveliest gift of all. He offers her an egg-shaped rock.

The rock part is mine. I made it up right here and now, hauling manure with the June sun shining down on me. I plan to put the rock Joshua gave me at the millpond in my dower chest, which Mrs. McDowell calls a hope chest, for that's its Virginia name. And I will pass my rock on for generations in my family to ponder—is it a geode? I think it is. I think it's a geode full of beautiful white crystals.

I smile at Jed as he opens the garden gate for me. He scowls back. He's upset over the way I blushed at Joshua this morning when I passed him a plate of hard-boiled eggs. Jed said it looked peculiar, seeing as how I am a Yankee and dressed as a boy.

But I am a girl inside—I am—and this girl likes that Joshua. *He kissed me.* With the sweet scent of white roses in the air, I push the wheelbarrow full of manure past Jed, the rows of bright green peas and over to Mrs. McDowell. Even in old work clothes, she wears one of those black crepe rosettes she and the prayer group ladies have made as badges of mourning for Stonewall Jackson. I dump the manure along the garden edge that's next to her row of tomato plants. Mrs. McDowell shades her eyes. She stares past me to the house. Something is causing dust to rise up from the lane. *Someone's coming.*

It's Uncle Butler, the man who helps Joshua tend Miss Adelaide's pigs. Uncle Butler is small and thin, with dark brown skin and bushy gray hair. He's helping Joshua out of a cart pulled by Buckshot, that pony who caused Private Hardin to do a somersault and break his leg. Clumsy Joshua. He's hurt himself again. His left foot is badly swollen and bruised.

"He done dropped a pail of pig slops on it," Uncle Butler explains as he and I help Joshua hobble into the house.

"Mercy me!" Mrs. McDowell bustles alongside us like a little hen dressed in black while Jed, keeping his distance as usual, brings up the rear. "What am I going to do with you, Joshua? You must be more careful!"

"I was careful, Grandmother." Joshua winces as he sits down on a kitchen chair. "That greedy pig, Patrick Henry, knocked the pail clean out of my hand. That's what made it fall on my foot."

"You gonna work around pigs, you best wear shoes," Uncle Butler says.

"Shoes should be coming momentarily," Mrs. McDowell says. I didn't know Joshua was meant to get a pair! Jed pokes me in the back. I ignore him. I didn't order those shoes. And where is Mister Eli anyway? He should have come to Faraway by now. I hope he's all right. I hope nothing called war got in his way. He said he'd order those shoes for the end of May and here we are—it's the second of June.

The next day, Jed and I are in Mrs. McDowell's potting shed soaking seed corn in coal tar and then coating it in plaster. This process makes the seed corn so disgusting, no crow will want to eat it. In the middle of this messy job, Mrs. McDowell bustles into the shed and says, "That sutler friend of yours has finally arrived!"

No sooner do I shout, "Mister Eli!" than Jed is off and running to the house to greet him. I stay behind to casually ask Mrs. McDowell, "Did Mister Eli bring those items you ordered?"

"He most certainly did! You'll never know how much this means to me, Adam." She takes my tarred hand between her two clean ones and gives it a loving squeeze. "I can't thank you enough. Oh Adam, it is always such a heartache, having loved ones fighting in a war. But . . ." Her eyes fill with tears. "But you already know that."

Yes I do. I am running now—my bare feet pounding the hard dry soil. I run around the side of Mrs. McDowell's large white house, dodging chickens scratching in the dirt and startling Dixie who, saddled and bridled, is tied to the dogwood where I first saw Joshua. Why is Dixie saddled? Always before, she was hitched to Mister Eli's wagon. There's Mister Eli—sitting on the front porch with Pa while Jed hovers over them like a little buzzard!

"Mister Eli! What happened to your wagon?" I climb the three porch steps and stop to catch my breath.

"He sold it!" Jed kicks a porch pillar with his bare foot. "Mister Eli sold his wagon because he's not going to be a sutler anymore. Mister Eli is leaving us!"

"Dear Adam! How good to see you." Mister Eli ignores Jed's outburst. Mister Eli takes my tarry hand and gives it a hearty shake. Then he lets go and rubs his palm on the sides of his trousers. He says, "I'm only going as far as Maryland—a fine border state that doesn't seem to know if it's allied with the North or South. I've always felt more comfortable there. Do you know what I plan to operate in Baltimore? An oyster bar! I have hopes that Roscoe will join me once this dreadful war is over."

"Have you news of the war?" Pa asks. Jed and I draw closer. In a low voice, Mister Eli says, "No. And that's what's so troubling. No one seems to know what's going on to the south of us. It's as if General Lee and his army have disappeared.

"However, there are rumors." Mister Eli always seems to have a stack of rumors. He's such a storyteller. "Rumors say Lee's army has crossed the Rappahannock River. Rumors have that army marching north across Virginia. They could be headed here."

"I knew this would happen!" Jed slams his hands against his thighs. Jed starts pacing across the back porch while slamming his thighs and I start picking tar from my hands. I had hoped that with Stonewall Jackson's death this would all be over. Jed says, "Lee's Army of Northern Virginia is headed here! Lee's army will join forces with the Gray Man here. They'll blow us up and then all go on to Winchester and win it back for the glory of the Confederacy!"

"Jed! Hush!" Pa grabs Jed's arm.

"My dear Jed. These are rumors." Mister Eli turns my little brother so that Jed faces him. "But if they turn out to be true, there is someone who can help you."

"You, Mister Eli?" I thought he was leaving for Maryland. He says, "Unfortunately, no. The man you want is Chaplain McCabe at Fort Milroy—only five miles away. He's with the Ohio One Hundred Twenty-second and is one of the finest, most upstanding men I know."

"He taught you the 'Battle Hymn of the Republic.' " I remember.

"Sir," Pa says to Mister Eli. I would not call him *sir*, but my pa does. "Do *you* think Lee's headed in this direction?"

"I don't know. But take heart, my good man. Chances are Lee will skip the Winchester area all together! I'm told he may once again have his eyes set farther north—on the lush Pennsylvania farmland. That's where he might head next—Pennsylvania."

"Pennsylvania is my home." Pa grips the edges of the chair he's sitting on. He grips them so tightly, I fear the chair will break. He struggles to stand. He grabs his crutches. He stands up so tall. My pa stands taller than any man I know. He hitches himself down the three porch steps. On crutches, he walks across the lawn and heads down the lane leading out from Faraway. Looking back at us, he shouts, "I must get well! I must protect my home!"

THIRTY TWO

THERE ARE TWO PATIENTS in the parlor now—Pa and Joshua. My dear pa walked farther today than he should have and he broke open the wound on his stump. I soothe it with a bath of Live-forever. I tell Pa, "Remember, you won't have to walk the whole way to Pennsylvania. You have Samson. In less than three weeks, you can travel home on Samson."

"Mein Gott! This healing takes too much time!" Pa's face looks white and strained. I hate war! Hate what it's done to Pa—done to us all. And now, if rumors are true, Lee could be bringing *war* to Pennsylvania.

We'll stop Lee. We did before at Antietam, Maryland. At that horrible battle where Sybil Freeman's father died.

After Pa, I tend to Joshua. I treat his injury with the essence of wormwood that Mrs. McDowell prepared because, she says, in cases such as Joshua's, wormwood works best. "I need *something* to help this foot," Joshua grumbles. "I have folks dependent on me."

By folks Joshua must mean Miss Adelaide, Uncle Butler and that pig Joshua talks about, Patrick Henry.

"When you work around greedy pigs, it's a good idea to wear shoes." I gently run a wet cloth over Joshua's swollen foot and around his heel.

"I like going barefoot." Joshua puts his hand on my short hair. Curling a strand of my hair around a finger, Joshua says, "One day I'll repay all your kindness, Anna Sunday." *He called me Anna.* "You remember that, you hear?"

Joshua is such a prince!

The next morning, however, Joshua is nowhere to be found and neither is Samson. Joshua, my prince, has repaid my kindness by stealing Samson. And why has Joshua done such a horrible thing? To deliver those shoes I ordered.

"Joshua will only go as far as his mother's house in Strasburg," Mrs. McDowell assures us. She's as upset as we are with Joshua. He's stolen Pa's one means of going home to Pennsylvania where, as Mrs. McDowell has often said, us Sundays belong. "I guarantee you, within four days, that fool boy will have your Samson back." She slams her hand against the parlor table. "I guarantee it."

Joshua McDowell is nothing. No thing. Not even a puff of wind against my neck on this hot June day. To think I'd considered him a prince. Joshua, who Mrs. McDowell said would be back in four days, has been gone a week!

With Mrs. McDowell's old hoe, I break up clods of hard dry garden soil so that her tomato plant roots can breathe. Why do I do this? Out of *charity*. I blush to think that, out of *charity,* I soothed Joshua's foot with the essence of wormwood.

"He'll be back any day now," Mrs. McDowell keeps saying.

Jed says we'll never see Joshua or Samson again. Jed says that after delivering shoes to his barefoot kin, Joshua joined the Army of Northern Virginia. "Right now, he's got Samson hitched to a wagon in front of a cave," Jed said earlier today. "Joshua's helping a Gray Man fill the wagon with niter."

"Niter? What is niter? Who has ever heard of niter?" I said.

"I have," Jed said. "Richard Townsend has. He wrote about niter in a book on explosives I found this morning tucked up high on a shelf. Niter's made from that white stuff in caves. Bat droppings, lime and rotten vegetables. Niter is used to make gunpowder. And you know what that can do." When I didn't answer, he said, "It blows up people."

I said, "Well that's just the most ridiculous thing I ever heard, Jed Sunday. Joshua would never use Samson to pull a wagon loaded with niter! Joshua knows we need our horse here so we can take Pa home.

"I'll tell you what's happened." I have thought about this a good long while and this is what I have decided. "Joshua and Samson got lost. So Joshua depended on our Bible horse to show him the way. Samson meandered a little and then, finally, reached a raging river he and Joshua must cross to return here.

"Now Joshua has learned many of Samson's Bible

commands from listening to you and me. Joshua also knows, because I told him, that there's a certain Yankee song Samson loves. It gives our horse the courage to face the unfaceable, which, for Samson, is that raging river.

"However, I never told Joshua the name of that song." Wish I had. "So I see Samson sitting on his hindquarters on the riverbank. And Joshua's trying to raise Samson up by singing him every Yankee song that he knows how. And those Joshua doesn't know? Why, he'll just have to learn them somehow. He's bound to hit the right one—sooner or later."

THIRTY THREE

It's a fitful Friday—
June 12. Earlier this morning, it rained. Now a bright sun shines. Joshua has been gone eight days. A lonely Miss Pete nestles against Pa's good leg. He paints the *Katherine* chest while Miss Pete keeps her eye pinned on the distant horizon—that wooded ridge. She looks so intently at it, I almost expect to see my beloved flash of dappled gray trotting through the trees with Joshua.

I smell roses on the wind as Jed and I shell peas on the back porch with Miss Pete and Pa. I also smell the linseed oil Pa mixes with the pigments we brought him from home. He uses these to paint his beautiful scenes on that base coat of milk paint.

Pa looks up from the wing tip of a dove he's painting. Flanked by two panels showing scenes of our home and beneath the keyhole of the *Katherine* chest, Pa has painted a dove. In the middle of the dove Pa has printed:

Faraway
1863

"Joshua will bring Samson back." Pa says what's been on our minds all morning. We've been searching the horizon for signs of Joshua all morning. He *will* come back. And there's that scent of roses again.

"Jed?" Pa says.

Gloomy Jed looks up from his colander of peas. Pa points his paintbrush at a little workbench, a *schnitzelbank,* he's painted in our barnyard on a side panel of the *Katherine* chest. Pa sings out—"Iss das not en schnitzelbank?"

He's singing the first line of our favorite song at home—the happy Schnitzelbank Song! Jed's supposed to answer by singing out the next line. Jed stares stone-faced at our pa. So I sing out the line instead—"Yah, das iss en schnitzelbank!"

"Iss das not en hinkel feder?" Pa points to Miss Pete because, of course, *hinkel feder* means chicken feather.

"Ya, das iss en hinkel feder!" I answer.

"Schnitzelbank, hinkel feder, ei du scheenie, ei du scheenie, ei du scheenie schnitzelbank!" Pa and I sing the chorus while I give silent Jed a pleading look—*can't we have a little fun on this fitful day? Please, join in.*

Now there are sixteen questions that Pa always sings out in our own peculiar version of the Schnitzelbank Song. There are sixteen answers we sing back. After the third question, Jed can't help but sing with us. Our fun Pa leads Jed and me through a rousing singing of the entire schnitzelbank song ending with the fertile goose:

> Iss das not en fertile goose?
> Ya, das iss en fertile goose!

Iss das not en ox rear end?
Ya das iss en ox rear end!
Fertile goose, ox rear end, abi schlopp
    schwartzl grop. . . .

Something about the sound of the words *abi schlopp* and *schwartzl grop* strikes me funny and I start to laugh. A moment later, Jed's laughing, too. Pa keeps right on singing with a fluffed-out Miss Pete waddling back and forth in front of him. It strikes me then how completely happy I am at this moment—with laughter, the Schnitzelbank Song, the sun on Faraway's back porch, the smell of Pa's paint and those roses on the wind.

And so, I am completely unprepared for what comes next. I am unable even to brace myself when the back door opens and Mrs. McDowell says, "I hate to interrupt all this. I am so sorry. I am so dreadfully sorry. But Uncle Butler has just come from Miss Adelaide's with disturbing news. Abraham, I need to talk you alone. Children, go into the parlor and wait for us there."

Jed and I pace back and forth as we wait for Pa and Mrs. McDowell. I count the roses in the parlor rug to make sure there are still nine. Nine is a sign of good things to come. I count the nine roses in the rug over and over, because it takes my mind off Jed who keeps on saying, "The Gray Man in the DANGEROUS BACKWOODS is about to blow us up."

When Mrs. McDowell and Pa finally appear, Pa sits Jed and me down on either side of him, which is not a good sign. Pa holds my right hand. Pa holds Jed's left. Mrs.

McDowell stands at Pa's right shoulder—her dress, so black against the tan homespun shirt he has on. Pa says to Jed and me, "We Sundays are all strong bricks, are we not?"

"Yes, Pa," we answer.

"We can take the hottest fires, for we know these fires just make us stronger?" he says.

"Yes, Pa," we say.

"Good. You must remember this always. Now, listen closely, for we have little time. Uncle Butler has a nephew. This nephew has seen thousands upon thousands of Rebel soldiers pouring through Chester's Gap—only twenty-five miles south of here. He says they are not the soldiers who have been in the valley for months pestering the Union Army, but the Army of Northern Virginia. Lee's army is on the move. Uncle Butler's nephew saw column after column. They march north—toward here. They have rifles and artillery—big guns. Howitzers. Parrott guns. My dear children, I need you to go to a place where I know you will be safe."

"But Pa," I say.

"No! Let me finish. You must pack your bags. Quickly. Uncle Butler will lead you through the woods behind Faraway. Uncle Butler knows a safe way—paths that will take you north to the Union camp. There you are to ask for Chaplain McCabe. Ask him to find you shelter in the main fort. Insist he put you in the main fort! It has high parapets and a bomb-proof to protect you from attack. Anna, do not let them know you're a girl. They might separate you from Jed. You must stick together."

"What about you?" I grip Pa's hand.

"I cannot walk to Winchester on crutches."

"We can't go without you!" I say.

"Mrs. McDowell will take good care of me."

"But Pa, you're not safe here," Jed says. I expect him to go on about the Gray Man, but no. Instead, my troublesome little brother says in a low voice, "Mrs. McDowell is a Rebel and she keeps a pistol beneath the pillow on her bed."

"This he knows." Mrs. McDowell answers for Pa.

"She's got a telescopic rifle!" Jed says.

"This he knows, too." Mrs. McDowell says each word as crisply as a whip snaps air.

"Does Pa know that Mrs. McDowell shot him with that telescopic rifle?" Jed says out loud and to my horror. Pa covers his face with his hands.

"She did not!" I say out loud right back. "That rifle is broken!" I look up at Mrs. McDowell for confirmation. *Say that it's broken.* Her pale green eyes fix on mine. The expression in them softens. Her eyes fill with so much love it brings tears to mine. She puts her hand on my shoulder. She says, "I will protect your father with my life. You know that, don't you?"

"Yes, I do." I press my cheek against her hand.

"That's my Anna. Jed, listen to Anna." Pa reaches over and he hugs me. He says, "My sweet Anna, my apple-dumpling queen." I rub my cheek against his thick soft beard and recall a vow I made one long ago night—*if I don't get Pa home, I will never be Anna Sunday again.* And now, Uncle Butler is shouting from the back door, "Ain't them children ready yet?"

193

PART FOUR

The Second Battle of Winchester

(June 12–15, 1863)

THIRTY FOUR

PACKED CARPETBAGS flung over our shoulders, Jed and I race after Uncle Butler, hustling down the green field behind the house at Faraway. Jed leaps across the little stream bordering the backwoods. I stop for one last look at the Rebel house where I've spent the past six weeks. The windows in the upper story reflect the afternoon sun. They look as if they are on fire.

Tears streaming down my face, I run after Jed. I shout at him, "Chaplain McCabe will send a wagon for Pa."

Jed stops. Jed turns. Jed shouts at me, "This is all your fault! If you hadn't ordered shoes, Joshua wouldn't have stolen Samson! Pa could be with us now—on Samson! You're just a silly girl! Girls ruin everything!"

"They do not!" I shout back. Jed takes off after Uncle Butler. Running beside Jed, I shout at his big left ear, "*This girl* bargained with a sutler to take us to Winchester. *This girl* saved you from One-Eyed Pete! *This girl* made shoofly pies. . . ." I stumble over a rock, which knocks the remaining words out of me—*this girl* is kind. Stumbling after Jed, I enter the deep shade of Jed's DANGEROUS BACKWOODS. A sudden, distant volley of rifle fire makes my heart leap inside me.

"Keep low!" Uncle Butler shouts. We duck down. We scramble through underbrush, up a hill and over a wooded ridge. We descend into a deep ravine to put the rifle fire behind us. We head north, following the ravine. I don't complain about our fast pace even though I'm hot and breathing hard. I climb over a stone fence without falling over it the way Joshua once did. I race across a wheat field faster than Jed, and when we hear distant rifle fire again, I pull him into a protecting patch of woods. Girls can go off to see the elephant, too.

The sound of distant rifle fire tails us most of the way to Winchester—*don't let that rifle fire reach Pa*. By the time we mount a ridge that overlooks the Union encampment, it is early evening and the rifle fire has finally ceased. Thousands upon thousands of tents are spread out on the slope below us with cooking fires spitting smoke and sparks into the dusky sky. A bugle blares. A group of mounted soldiers gallops into camp, stirring up a whirlwind of smoke and dust.

"This is as far as I go." Uncle Butler takes off his cap. With his arm, he wipes the sweat off his forehead. "You can see your way from here?"

"We go there." I point to an enclave of tents over on the far left of the encampment. I remember them from the time I visited Mister Eli.

"Now you're gonna be just fine and your daddy is, too." Uncle Butler puts his hands on our shoulders. "You're good Yankees." Uncle Butler squeezes our shoulders and then releases them. "You go on now. And don't you let no army—Union or Rebel—get you so low you don't do nothin'. You always got to do something. You do what I always tell Joshua—*root, hog, or die!*"

"Root, hog, or die!" I shout. I like the sound of it. I *will* be a rooting hog. I'll alert the Union Army that General Robert E. Lee is coming. I'll have a wagon sent for Pa. I'll get Pa home—*root, hog, or die!*

Jed and I race downhill to the Union encampment. I lead Jed through long aisles formed by tents, and past hanging cooking pots that bubble with something that smells like rotten dandelion greens. I find Chaplain McCabe's tent and it's not even dark yet. Only dusk and Chaplain McCabe, who has dark hair and sparkling brown eyes, is about to leave for town to sing in a quartet for General Milroy. General Lee's Army of Northern Virginia is about to attack and the chaplain is going into town to sing! As he fastens the brass buttons on his blue coat, I quickly explain to him who Jed and I are—friends of Mister Eli and children of Private Abraham Sunday, who was badly injured, but is almost better now.

"He's staying five miles south of here—at a Rebel house," I tell the chaplain. "He's in danger! You've got to send a horse and wagon for him now! You've got to bring him to the fort right now!"

"General Robert E. Lee is headed toward him and this encampment, too!" Jed waves his arms at the surrounding tents. "You've got to stop Lee!"

"Now boys," Chaplain McCabe says, which brings me up short. Being with Pa has softened me into being his

Anna. I am Adam once again. *I will not forget it.* "If a force that large were approaching, General Milroy would have heard about it."

"General Milroy doesn't know Lee's army is headed here?" I ask. He must know it's headed here! He's a general! Generals are SUPPOSED TO KNOW! "Uncle Butler's nephew saw thousands of Rebels pouring through Chester's Gap! They have guns!"

"Big guns! Artillery!" Jed holds out his arms to show how big these guns are.

For a moment, Chaplain McCabe looks as if he believes us. Then he frowns. Then he says, "How can this be? A reconnoitering party rode through that area only today. They encountered no Rebel artillery. Only cavalry. The prisoners they took were only cavalry troops that have been skulking in the area for months."

"No!" Jed says. "It's not those skulking Rebels gathering niter in the BACKWOODS! It's General Lee's army! I know! My pa knows! He told Adam and me to stay in the fort. It's the one place we'll be safe from howitzers and big guns like that!"

The chaplain puts his hands on our shoulders the way that Uncle Butler did. But the chaplain doesn't say, *"Root, hog, or die!"* He says, "There's nothing for you to be alarmed about. Lee could not possibly be headed here. His army's still reeling from Chancellorsville.

"But I *will* mention what you said to General Milroy. Meanwhile, I'll have my cook Willie escort you to the fort. You can stay in the fort tonight. Mrs. Houseknecht will take you in. That laundry woman is worth her weight in gold. Tomorrow, we'll contact Chaplain Eberhart of the Pennsylvania Eighty-seventh about your father. By tomorrow afternoon, we should have him safely here." The chaplain pats our backs as if to say everything's all right.

"There's nothing to be alarmed about," he repeats.

"But we heard rifle fire!" I say.

"What you heard was our men skirmishing with Rebel cavalry. No troops are amassing or General Milroy would have heard about it. I guarantee it. Now cheer up, be hopeful and look on the bright side. All will be well."

The main fort stands on a high ridge overlooking the Union encampment where Chaplain McCabe has his tent. The fort has no roof. But it does have steep earthen walls surrounding it. The walls have rifle pits in front of them for soldiers to hide in as they fire their guns at the approaching enemy. However, no soldiers are manning these rifle pits right now, because, of course, no one seems to know that a huge enemy is approaching.

There are officers' quarters and barracks for the enlisted men outside the fort and not far from the main gate. I expect this is where Mrs. Houseknecht, the laundry woman, will have her tent. But no. "Yesterday, she moved everything inside the fort," Willie, the chaplain's cook, explains. "She thinks same as you—trouble's coming." He grins at me.

"I wouldn't grin if I were you," I say.

"We know a lot of things you don't," Jed says.

"All you know are rumors." Willie shows his pass to a guard at the gate who waves us through into the fort itself. It feels as large as our back field where Samson likes to graze with the cows. Only, instead of fences, the fort has those high earthen walls surrounding it and there is no grass in sight. Up close, I see that the walls are made of earth, stone and logs, piled one on top of the other. They form the large figure of a diamond with big guns lined up along the sides.

Jed and I follow Willie down a sort of alleyway between the fort's rear wall and what looks like some kind of large partly underground shelter made of stone and earth. Gripping my bag, I feel the reassuring shape of Cousin Ezekiel's pocket Bible, which I packed inside. From the fort's main gate a sentinel calls out—"Post number one. It's seven o'clock and all is well." Other sentinels pick up the cry:

"All is well. All is well. All is well."

THIRTY FIVE

MRS. HOUSEKNECHT IS no fool. She knows something's about to happen. Yesterday, her aching hip bones told her there's trouble in the air, so she had her husband move her up here to the fort. She has set up camp in an out of the way corner at the rear of the fort. Her small tent, next to a large cistern where a laundress can get all the water she needs, is protected by the fort's high wall.

"I have to keep my Billy-Bobs safe," the large red-faced woman tells Jed and me. By Billy-Bobs, she means her six-year-old twins, Billy and Bob, who squirm in the grip of her red and peeling laundry woman's hands. The Billy-Bobs have short, sturdy legs, round red faces and it's hard to tell one from the other—except that Billy has a mole underneath his right earlobe.

"You just tell anyone who asks—you belong with Mrs. Houseknecht and her boys," she says. She's so kind. She says, "You're Jed and Adam Houseknecht now!"

"We are?" Houseknecht is an odd-sounding name.

She says, "You don't want to be unclaimed boys, do you? Unclaimed boys get thrown out of the fort on their un-claimed rear ends!

"Your new father is an artillery man!" Mrs. House-knecht says. "He's off playing cards right now. Would you like to see his cannon? It's a fifteen-inch Rodman Columbiad—the largest cannon in Fort Milroy!

"Harold is the number one man on the gun crew!" Mrs. Houseknecht explains as she leads us across a wide open space inside the fort. Above us, stars are popping out across the sky. Is Pa looking at the stars? I wish my pa were here. Mrs. Houseknecht says, "After the big gun is fired, the number one man sponges out the cannon bore to remove any remaining sparks."

"If a spark stays inside the cannon and you try to load it, watch out! That gun will blow up in your face—ka-boom!" a Billy-Bob says.

"Pow-pow-pow!" the other Billy-Bob screams.

"Pow-pow-pow!" Jed repeats with such fierceness, it scares me. He tears off with the Billy-Bobs toward the huge cannon mounted on an iron carriage next to a flag-pole that must stand fifty feet high. Mrs. Houseknecht, as large as she is, looks dwarfed by this tall flagpole and the monster cannon beside it. She says, "General Milroy calls this cannon his *baby waker*."

I feel sorry for all the babies this cannon might awaken. Jed and the Billy-Bobs try to pick up one of the cannon-balls piled beside it, but the ball's so heavy, they can't budge it. I climb up on the *baby waker*'s iron carriage so that I can look out over the fort wall. The *baby waker* is aimed toward Winchester with its lanterns glowing so pretty in the distance.

I hate war.

"The *baby waker* can shoot those three-hundred-pound balls at targets up to three miles away," Mrs. Houseknecht tells Jed. He looks up at her, his eyes wide with awe.

"The fort's got a magazine full of ammunition and gunpowder to protect us from the dirty Rebels!" one of the Billy-Bobs tells Jed.

"I know about gunpowder." My brother stares hard at me. "They use niter to make it."

I hate niter.

"Want to see the powder magazine?" The Billy-Bobs grab Jed's hands. Staring at me Jed says, "Yes I do." The three of them tear off, but I don't follow them. I want nothing to do with gunpowder. Mrs. Houseknecht shouts after the three boys, "Now don't you go inside that powder magazine!" To me she says, "I can tell that you're the sensible brother. Would you like to see a bomb-proof? It's where we go if we're under attack."

A bomb-proof is the structure I passed on my way to Mrs. Houseknecht's tent. It's a sturdy structure built inside the fort to protect people from heavy gunfire—the kind the *baby waker* makes. A bomb-proof has snug-looking walls that are made of logs heavily banked with earth. It has a little door on the side and the roof is made of heavy logs covered with several feet of earth. It's the kind of underground place where Thumbelina might have stayed when she lived with the field mouse. It's the kind of place where she found the dying swallow.

"This is where I'd like to spend the night," I tell Mrs. Houseknecht. We are inside the roomy bomb-proof, which is not far from her tent. Through the bomb-proof's open door, I can see the sky beyond, filled with stars.

"But a bomb-proof is so damp and unwholesome. It's dirty!" Mrs. Houseknecht places her reddened hands on her large hips and frowns at me. "You don't want to be sleeping in here!"

"But I do." I want to be surrounded by the bomb-proof's sturdy darkness. I want to sleep in a corner, with a wall at my head and one at my side and pretend that I'm at home.

And I won't come out until the war is over.

At night, after a quick supper of hardtack soaked in water and fried in bacon grease, which Jed and I eat with the Billy-Bobs, Jed declares to me he's decided to sleep with the two boys in their tent. They'll stay up all night talking about Fort Milroy's *baby waker,* four twenty-pound Parrott rifled guns and two twenty-four-pound howitzers.

"Well good for you." I don't want to talk about anything that has to do with war. *"I'm* going to learn about farming and growing things." I snitch the *1863 Farmer's Almanac* Jed brought along with him and I stalk off to the bomb-proof. There, next to my bedroll, I set up a lantern Mrs. Houseknecht lent me. By my side, I place the rock that Joshua gave me because, for some strange reason, I can't give it up.

First, I read from Cousin Ezekiel's Bible Psalm 139—up through verse eighteen. I love these eighteen verses. They say God is with me even in the darkest night. Surely this will be a dark night—without Pa and the first I've ever slept apart from Jed.

Next, I open up the almanac. I decide to read May's article about birds and how beneficial they are to the farmer. As I am reading it, who should enter the bomb-proof? Jed! Without saying a word, my rutchety brother unrolls his bedroll on the dirt floor next to mine. He prefers me to the noisy Billy-Bobs?

I let several quiet moments pass and then, I read aloud to Jed from May's article about the helpful birds: " 'Who can estimate the number of insects they destroy?' " I read. " 'On a careful count it was found that one brood of birds destroyed not less than five hundred caterpillars a day, or about fifteen thousand a month.'

"Now that's a helpful fact," I tell Jed. "A farmer should know birds are helpful. Here's another. An angry farmer killed a quail because he thought it was eating his corn. Do you know what they found in that quail's craw? One cut worm, twenty-one striped vine-bugs and one hundred chinch bugs, but not a single kernel of corn. The poor quail was actually helping the farmer and the quail got shot.

"That was a tragic accident." I am thinking not only of the farmer and the quail, but also of Mrs. McDowell and Pa. *People make mistakes.*

"I want us to pray for Pa." Jed's thinking of Pa, too.

After the Lord's Prayer, I pray aloud to God to keep Pa safe so we can bring him to the fort tomorrow. I ask forgiveness for any mistakes I may have made. I ask forgiveness for mistakes others may have made as well. "Dear God," I pray, "I know from living with the enemy, it's mostly made up of ordinary people—some kind, some who make mistakes—like Mrs. McDowell."

Then Jed prays, "Dear God, make Mrs. McDowell worthy of trust even though she owns a telescopic rifle and she shot our pa with it. Make her take good care of Pa until we get him to Fort Milroy. And God? Help us to beat back Lee."

THIRTY
SIX
I AM DREAMING. IT'S A
nightmare. I am in a cave. I struggle against chains pin-
ning me against a cave's cold damp wall. I have to free
myself. I have to help Mrs. McDowell save Pa and they
are just beyond my reach. Encased in a protective bubble,
Pa lies prostrate on a cot while Mrs. McDowell, wielding
a cast-iron skillet, bravely tries to fight off a giant June
bug dressed in Confederate gray. The June bug's huge
black pincers reach over Mrs. McDowell to pop Pa's
bubble and seize him, and I shriek, waking myself up.

I am in a bomb-proof at Fort Milroy. It's barely dawn.
Jed's still sleeping. Reeling from the nightmare, I light
Mrs. Houseknecht's lantern. In its pale glow, I use the
rock Joshua gave me to write a note in the dirt of the
bomb-proof's floor—*Jed! Have gone to remind Chaplain
McCabe about Pa!* Chaplain McCabe needs to talk to
Chaplain Eberhart right now! He needs to send that
wagon for Pa NOW.

I need my pa here with me.

Except for soldiers milling about General Milroy's

baby waker, the fort is quiet. A sleepy sentry waves me through the gate. As I hurry past the officers' quarters, someone says, "We'll alert McReynolds. He knows the signal—two cannon shots."

Lee's coming!

I race downhill to the Union encampment. Unlike the fort, the encampment is wide-awake. Soldiers hurriedly drink coffee, strap on guns and saddle horses. I ask a soldier about to mount his trembling horse, "What's happening?"

"It's just Rebels startin' to put up a fuss." He swings up on his excited horse.

"But it's not just *some* Rebels. It's the Army of Northern Virginia!" I tell him and he laughs at me. From uphill at the main fort, a cannon fires twice. The soldier's horse rears with him and takes off at a run.

Dodging a platoon of marching soldiers, I run to Chaplain McCabe's tent. But he's not there. He's in town. "He'll talk to Chaplain Eberhart," Willie, the cook, reassures me. "But if you want to make sure, Chaplain McCabe will be back in an hour."

While I wait to talk to him, I try to keep my mind off Lee's advancing army by helping Willie with his chores. Soldiers gallop in and out of camp and barrages of distant rifle fire go on somewhere to the south. Willie insists its Rebel cavalry fighting our pickets. I insist it's General Lee. Willie refuses to believe me. No one believes me! By midmorning Chaplain McCabe still has not appeared and I must return to the fort. Jed will be worried.

"Don't you worry about your pa," Willie calls after

me. "At this very moment, he's probably in a wagon headed here."

Fort Milroy is not quiet now. Sergeants drill squads of marching men. Teams of soldiers hustle about the fort's big guns. Jed, standing off to one side of the *baby waker*, watches two soldiers, using tongs, place a cannonball inside the *baby waker's* mouth. High above the cannon, an officer with silver-gray hair, which doesn't match his dark beard and mustache, sits in a basket that's been hoisted to the top of the fifty-foot flagpole. With the stars and stripes fluttering overhead, the officer surveys the countryside far below through spyglasses pressed tightly against his face.

"Who's that?" I ask, running up to Jed.

"*The Silver Eagle,* General Milroy." Jed's face looks white and tense. "*The Silver Eagle's* deciding which target his *baby waker* should fire at first. He thinks it's Rebel cavalry he's firing at, Adam.

"Do you know what happens if one of Milroy's cannonballs hits an ammunition wagon? It blows sky-high!"

"Our pa could be out there in a wagon, Jed. Pa could get hurt," I say as, across the fort, a soldier barks, "Ready! *Baby waker!*" Oh no. They're going to fire that gun! I break into a run. Screaming, "Stop!" I sprint across the open space and toward the cannon. Someone yells, "Fire!" A soldier, facing backward, facing me, jerks a long wire. The *baby waker* erupts—*BAB-BOOM!* A deafening freight train of smoky air slams into me and lifts me off my feet! It slams me backward against the ground! I knock my back so hard against the ground, I can't breathe. I—can't breathe.

"Adam, are you all right?" I hear Jed say beside me.

"He'll be all right," a deep voice says through a loud ringing in my ears. *I can't breathe.* "Relax. Your breath will come." After a long and frantic moment, my breath does come. Gulping, I take great huge breaths of smoky air. And then, I cough and cough.

"The blast knocked you over." The man with the deep voice helps me to sit up. He has gold epaulettes on his shoulders. He's an officer. He says, "You should always stand to one side of a firing cannon.

"Who are you, son?"

"Adam Houseknecht," I remember to say.

"Our pa's the number one man on the *baby waker* crew," Jed says.

"I should think an artillery man's son would know where to stand when his father's gun is being fired." The officer helps me to my feet. Ahead of us, a stocky-looking soldier with a long ramrod sponges out the *baby waker's* smoking barrel. That soldier must be Jed's and my new pa.

They're going to fire that gun again.

"I need to tell my pa something really important." My real pa could be out there. My real pa could get hurt.

"Not now." The officer brushes off the seat of my pants. "Why aren't you wearing shoes?"

I look down at my bare feet. I wore Cousin Ezekiel's brogans to get to the Union camp. But then I took them off because they hurt me. I haven't put them on since.

"A fort with firing artillery is no place for bare feet."
With one hand firmly on my shoulder and the other on
Jed's, the officer escorts us away from the big guns and
over to Mrs. Houseknecht's tent. "This isn't a summer
picnic going on at Winchester," he says.

"This is war."

THIRTY SEVEN

AND WAR IT IS. Rebel cavalry (that's what everyone calls it) drives in our Union pickets and the Rebels advance north to within four miles of Winchester! General Milroy sends out soldiers to fight them off. Gunfire goes on to the south of us all morning. General Milroy's big guns often join the fray—belching fire and smoke as they shoot cannonballs south to cover our Union soldiers as they retreat to higher ground.

"Don't you fret. The Rebs ain't nothing we can't handle," Private Houseknecht tells Jed and me when the private comes to check on us at noon. "Don't fret about your pa, neither. No chaplain in his right mind would send a wagon south for him through all the commotion. Once it's over, they'll fetch him for you. He'll be all right. You boys, too. Just stay in the bomb-proof and out of harm's way."

During the long hot afternoon, Jed and I stand an uneasy vigil at the bomb-proof's door while Mrs. Houseknecht, in the rear, plays cards with the Billy-Bobs to keep them occupied. Each time General Milroy, high in his flagpole basket, gestures for one of his big guns to fire, Jed and I alert Mrs. Houseknecht.

She gathers in her sturdy little boys and covers their ears. Once the firing of our big guns ceases and there is an equally deafening silence peppered now and again by distant rifle fire, Mrs. Houseknecht says loud enough for Jed and me to hear, "Now my Billy-Bobs. Do we hear any Rebel artillery firing back at us?"

"No, Mama," the Billy-Bobs answer. "Just some puny rifle fire—*rat-a-tat*." And she says, "And what does this tell us?"

"That those dirty Rebs don't have big guns like ours. Only little ones. So it can't be the Army of Northern Virginia like Jed and Adam think." They look at us when they say this.

"And where are the big guns that keep us safe?" she asks her Billy-Bobs.

"At Fort Milroy, Star Fort, West Fort, Bowers Hill . . ." The boys recite these fortifications around Winchester the way Jed and I would Pa's litany about bricks. The Billy-Bobs' litany seems to comfort them. I won't be comforted until the firing's stopped and I have Pa beside me.

During a lull in the firing of the big guns, I slip outside the bomb-proof to get fresh air. Horses brought into the fort for safety mill about. Horses snort at the cannon smoke that hangs over the fort and makes the whole place smell like rotten eggs. Through this smoke, I see a dappled gray horse hitched to a wagon near the main gate. Did Joshua return with Samson? Did Samson bring Pa here through all the fighting?

With Cousin Ezekiel's brogans flopping on my feet, I run through the heat and smoke toward our beautiful old horse. I knew I could trust that Joshua! I draw close to Samson and he turns his head. But it's not Samson. Pa's not in the wagon, either. Only some sutler's goods and . . . and two wounded soldiers. They cry out to me for water and, fighting back my tears, I bring them some.

At dusk, hundreds of soldiers pour into the fort for safety. Everyone still insists it's not General Lee attacking our Union stronghold. How could it be? Lee's army with its immense artillery and baggage trains could never have escaped from the Army of the Potomac and crossed the Blue Ridge! Everyone says, if it had, General Milroy would have been notified of it.

"He was notified!" I scream inside. But I say nothing out loud. I keep myself from thinking of Pa and what's going to happen now by fetching water for thirsty soldiers who are injured and can't walk.

Near the cistern, several surgeons set up a first aid station to treat the wounded. Not far from it, I discover a soldier with his back propped against the fort's rear wall. The soldier is as big as Pa was before he went off to see the elephant. The soldier has Pa's curly reddish-brown hair, and a bloodied kerchief is wrapped around his throat. I learn that this soldier who reminds me of Pa has a musket ball lodged in his throat and the surgeons can't do anything for him.

With a wet rag, I gently wash the soldier's face while avoiding the kerchief—freshly red. He is bleeding even now. I wash his hands and arms. When I finish, he touches my arm. His eyes plead—*bide with me a while.*

And so, I sit beside the soldier with the ball in his throat and read to him from Cousin Ezekiel's Bible. I read the first eighteen verses of Psalm 139 because they're my favorite (God is with you wherever you may go). My voice breaks as I read the verses I love the most: "Whither shall I go from thy spirit? Or whither shall I flee from thy presence? If I ascend into heaven, thou *art* there . . ." As I read, the soldier lays his hand on top of mine and he keeps it there. "Even there shall thy hand lead me, and thy right hand shall hold me. . . ."

Oh I am grateful for the soldier's hand on mine. Never have I been so close to war. Storm clouds gather in the dome of sky above Fort Milroy. I fear a terrible storm is about to erupt with General Lee's massive forces clashing against ours. The soldier is breathing hard as he tries to keep his own blood from choking him to death. There is a small but growing pile of amputated limbs next to the surgeons' first aid station—arms, legs and, now, a foot.

THIRTY EIGHT

In the glow of lamplight, Jed and I lay out our bedrolls in the corner of the bomb-proof that has become our home away from home. With the artillery quiet for the night, the Houseknechts have retreated to their tent; Jed and I have the bomb-proof to ourselves. Jed says General Milroy's big guns fired seventy—seventy!—shells to protect our regrouping soldiers today. And have I ever heard of a powder monkey? A powder monkey carries loads of gunpowder from the magazine to the cannon. He's a valuable member of the gun crew. Jed says, "A boy like me could be a powder monkey."

"You don't want to be a powder monkey. You don't want anything to do with war! People get hurt in war. People die!" I shout at him as someone knocks on the bomb-proof's door. It's Chaplain McCabe!

"A wagon wasn't sent for our pa; not in all this fighting," I say to him. He shakes his head, no. Thank God. Pa's safe—at least from cannonballs. Mrs. McDowell will keep him safe from everything else. She will!

The chaplain has on a white shirt stained with dirt and

blood and he carries a Bible underneath one arm. He looks at me with dark eyes that seem full of sadness, and regret.

"It's General Lee's army out there, isn't it," I say.

"We think it's only part of Lee's command," he says. "Stonewall Jackson's old command—the Second Corps of the Army of Northern Virginia led by General Richard S. Ewell."

"Then it's not *all* of Lee's army." That's some relief.

"Not at the moment." The chaplain's dark eyes study me. A gust of wind blows through the door he left open. We're going to have a storm. He says, "But if Ewell is spearheading the operation, Lee won't be far behind."

"Oh." Jed's eyes grow large and worried looking. Jed had *thought* it was Lee's army. Now, like me, Jed knows for sure. I put my arm around him.

"Don't worry." Chaplain McCabe tries to smile. "Our hopes are that after a little skirmishing, Lee's army will skirt Winchester. General Milroy is banking on it. We all know Lee wants to conserve his troops and ammunition. We all know he has his eyes set north on a larger, more important destination where his troops can grow strong feeding off the land."

"And what would that destination be?" I ask. My heart knows. Already my heart knows. Chaplain McCabe must see the pain in my eyes because he pauses before he says the name of my beloved state where Cousin Ezekiel waits for Samson to return to him with Pa and Jed and me— Pennsylvania.

It's late at night. Storm clouds that had gathered earlier are exploding now. Heaven's artillery has turned itself on

Jed and me. Thunder crashes down at us. Lightning stabs the dark patch of sky we see through the bomb-proof's door, which we've cracked open for fresh air. Bullets of rain assault our shelter. I hold Jed in my arms. He has his back to me. Jed whispers, "It's the end of the world."

"It's just a storm." I hug Jed close.

"It's the end of the world and it's all my fault," Jed whispers. "I broke our Holy Bible Pact. I spied on Joshua."

"I know that, Jed." I've sensed it all along.

"God's mad," Jed says.

"God knows people make mistakes, Jed. That's why God invented forgiveness; God forgives us." I try to turn Jed around so that he faces me. He burrows his back into my stomach and pulls my arms back around him. Jed's confession comes out in hurried whispers between loud crashes of thunder. That day I went off without Jed to the Union camp, he trailed Joshua to a cave where the Gray Man gathered niter. It's what they use to make gun-powder, Jed says.

"I know that, Jed." I know all sorts of things now.

"Joshua gave the Gray Man a whole passel of letters!" Jed turns around to face me. His skin has turned so white, his freckles stand out like little polka dots. "Mrs. McDowell's prayer group friends wrote those letters—I think. I . . . I think they told the Rebels what our Union soldiers were up to in town. That's why those Rebels are headed here now."

"No, Jed. You can't believe this." I can't, either. "If you did, you would have told Pa."

"It would have brought on the end of the world for Pa.

He likes Mrs. McDowell, but still, he'd turn her and Joshua over to General Milroy because Pa loves our Union Army even more and then, General Milroy would put Joshua and his grandmother on the side of the road with no food or water and General Milroy would send Pa to a hospital full of typhoid fever and us to an orphan home and the Union Army would take over Faraway. They'd eat Miss Pete . . ." Jed bursts into tears.

"Oh Jed." I take him in my arms.

"There's more." Between sobs, Jed tells me that after Joshua delivered those letters, he ran off to Miss Adelaide's. She gave Joshua a package and he ran off someplace else but Jed couldn't follow because he had to get back to Pa. Before Jed did, he stopped to visit with Miss Adelaide's pigs—mostly Yorkshire whites, but none as handsome as our Lauden Honor. The pigs talked so loudly to Jed he didn't hear Miss Adelaide coming up behind him. She grabbed the back of Jed's neck and spun him around. "Don't shoot!" Jed said and she said, "Who are you that I shouldn't shoot you?" Jed said, "I am Jed Sunday, the son of Abraham Sunday who got shot trying to save your Patrick Henry." She said, "Lord have mercy on us. Jed Sunday! Kate didn't mean to shoot your daddy. You do know that, don't you?"

"Kate as in Katherine McDowell," Jed says. "That telescopic rifle in her garret was never broken, Adam. And now Mrs. McDowell, who shot our pa, could be turning him over to General Lee's army as we speak. Pa could already be a prisoner as we speak. Do you know where Rebels take prisoners like Pa? To Castle Thunder!"

"No, Jed! That prison's only for civilians. Mister Eli

said so. Besides, Mrs. McDowell loves Pa like a son. She said she'd protect him with her life and I . . . I believe her!"

"That telescopic rifle was never broken," Jed repeats.

"I know that, Jed." Deep inside, I've known it all along. I just didn't want to face it out loud and in front of everyone. But that was the Anna part of me. Silly Anna. She also helped Mrs. McDowell order shoes for barefoot Rebels. And why did Anna do this? Because she believed in impossible things like kindness and fairy-tale princes.

THIRTY NINE

ALL IS QUIET THE NEXT morning. The storm has ceased. Half-asleep, I stumble outside the bomb-proof; I want to check on the soldier with the ball in his throat. But he's not where I left him the night before—propped against the rear fort wall. A soldier with his arm in a sling sits there now. When I ask, he says they took the other soldier away. "To the Taylor House?" I've heard this is where the Union Army takes many of its wounded; it's a house in town.

"You could call it that," the soldier says in a way that tells me he's trying to be kind. He doesn't want to say right out that the man with the ball in his throat has died.

I walk back to the bomb-proof with a horrible lump in my throat. I sit against a pile of wet sandbags, hug my knees and watch a hot sun slowly burn off clouds. Joining me, Jed stares up at that silent sky and says what's on my worried mind as well, "Where's Lee?"

A little later, distant rifle fire erupts to the south of the fort. Mrs. Houseknecht says she can tell by the sound that those faraway rifles aren't aimed at the fort. She says even if they were, no bullet could penetrate the fort's thick walls.

"Of course, a cannonball could and that's why General Milroy keeps a close watch out for enemy artillery." She points to the general, back up in his flagpole basket. "If any part of Lee's army threatens the fort, *the Silver Eagle* will alert us. We'll take shelter in our sturdy bomb-proof while his big guns defend us."

I fetch firewood for Mrs. Houseknecht from behind the officers' quarters while keeping a wary eye on *the Silver Eagle*. Through his spyglasses, he scans the shimmering horizon for signs of the enemy. General Milroy will keep us safe.

The Billy-Bobs, wound as tight as corkscrews, run toward me shouting, "Carry us, Adam!" They wrap their arms around my legs and put their bare feet on top of mine. In spite of yesterday's warning, both the Billy-Bobs and I are barefoot. With an armload of firewood and a Billy-Bob on either leg, I slog over to Mrs. Houseknecht. She's about to heat water to do her laundry—life must go on.

"Don't bring me any little boys right now," she says. "Why don't all of you go play a game? Adam, could you find a game to keep my boys occupied?" She looks apologetically at me. She knows how anxious I am feeling.

There is a yard-wide puddle in our corner of the fort and I decide we'll play "jump the puddle." From the puddle, I can see General Milroy; I can keep my eye on him.

The object of the puddle game is to see who can clear the puddle by the greatest distance. Jed declares that since my legs are the longest, I must begin my jump one yard before the puddle starts to make the contest fair and equal. Jed's anxious, but trying not to show it.

With trouser legs rolled up to the knees I run, run, run and then I leap—farther, farther, farther—to land, barefoot, splat, into the wet soft mud. The longer we play the puddle game, the farther I leap—my bare feet slapping mud. Pounding mud. Slipping through mud. Mud between the toes. Mud on my heels. Nothing hurts. This is fun. This feels good. *Joshua would like this.*

Joshua. I stop dead and the hurt slams into me. *Joshua betrayed me.* He betrayed us all. Pa's stuck at Faraway. Jed and I are here. The Army of Northern Virginia could be just about anywhere. Suddenly, what I want to do most is go inside the bomb-proof and cry. But here are Jed and the Billy-Bobs, all excited by the puddle game and covered in mud.

"Let's make the puddle a pond," I tell them. "We'll use empty sardine cans for boats—"

"We'll turn them into Rebel boats and bomb them!" a Billy-Bob shrieks.

"Remember that little boat called Glory?" Jed says as we float sardine cans that the Billy-Bobs bomb with an arsenal of pebbles. "Where do you think Glory went?"

"Glory's with our pa, Jed." I like to think that they're together, and once this war is over, Mrs. McDowell will bring Pa and Glory home.

And now, a bugle blares—*to arms.* General Milroy shouts to his men. I hear the distant rumble of artillery. A ball of light streaks overhead. It rattles. It bursts—exploding across the sky. "That's Rebel artillery!" Mrs. Houseknecht screams. "They're firing at us! Get inside the bomb-proof now!"

I'm scared. Thirty of us have crammed ourselves into the hot, dark bomb-proof—thirty of us!—the House-knechts, Jed, a group of twenty-five laundry women with children and me. A laundry woman I can't see because it's so dark in here keeps reciting Psalm 46—"God is our refuge and our strength. . . ." Each time we hear the whine of an approaching enemy shell, she screams, "Prepare yourself to die!"

I put my hands over the ears of a screaming Billy-Bob and pray—"Our father who art in Heaven . . ." I pray to Our Father all morning while enemy shells I can't see scream overhead. Each time a shell explodes, the earth trembles beneath me. I fear our sturdy shelter of earth and logs will collapse on us. I grow so tired from all the fearing. My stomach aches.

At noon, the shelling ceases.

Because I'm the oldest *boy* and a *brave boy* at that (our Adam didn't scream once; our Adam's a prince, Mrs. Houseknecht tells everyone), she sends me outside to find out what's been going on. Even with all the shelling, the fort's still standing. It looks as if it's hardly been hit!

A soldier corralling a runaway horse tells me the Rebels overtook the Union guns at Bowers Hill. "It's those big guns they've been firing at us," he says.

"Those guns are quiet now." The eerie quiet raises the hairs on the back of my neck.

"That's what's got us worried. Him, too." The soldier

points to General Milroy—up the flagpole and scanning the countryside to the south and east.

When Mrs. Houseknecht hears my news, she says, "We'll be all right. We've still got control of the main fort and the big guns at Star Fort and West Fort, too."

"Star Fort's got eight big guns," Jed whispers up at me. "West Fort has six. If we didn't have them to protect us, Fort Milroy would be an open duck."

"You mean a sitting duck," I whisper back.

"I mean a duck sitting out in the open with hundreds of Rebel cannons and thousands of rifles aimed at it. You know what happens to the duck then? It gets blown up!"

Well, I'm certainly glad we're not an open duck! I don't know what I'd do if I got blown up. How could I gather all my pieces? The eerie quiet goes on for several hours. I begin to think General Lee has sneaked past us. If he has, will our army stop him from invading Pennsylvania? It will! It stopped Lee before.

At three P.M., the shelling starts up all over again! Now the Rebels fire shells at us from what seems like all directions! Each time a shell shrieks overhead, it gives a death rattle as it bursts. As one frightening hour of shelling follows another, I feel as if I've died a thousand times and then, it's dusk. The shelling ceases.

With smoke clinging to the hot damp air and my ears still ringing from artillery fire, I learn the reason for the strange silence at noon. After overtaking the Union guns at Bowers Hill, and while General Milroy kept his eyes pinned to the south and east, a part of Lee's army quietly sneaked north and west. It overtook the Union guns at Star Fort and West Fort, too.

General Lee, with those thousands upon thousands of troops Uncle Butler's nephew saw pouring through Chester's Gap a few days ago, has us surrounded.

All around us, soldiers talk. Do we stay and defend the fort? But Lee's forces outnumber ours by thousands of men! Do we flee—under cover of darkness and, if need be, fight our way through the Confederate line to the Union garrison at Harper's Ferry?

At nine P.M. it's decided. Fort Milroy cannot be defended; our army must flee. *We must flee.* We can't leave anything of value behind! Jed and I help carry out ammunition. We dump it down a nearby well. The artillery, including General Milroy's *baby waker,* is spiked so that the Rebels can't fire it. Soldiers cut up wagon wheels and axles. I help Private Houseknecht break open cracker boxes and fill haversacks with food. I wonder how long it will take us to get to Harper's Ferry? Will we have to cross a mountain?

Jed and I gather our few belongings. We're ready to leave with General Milroy and his men. It's not until midnight we discover we won't be retreating to Harper's Ferry with them. "There could be fighting; you could get hurt," Private Houseknecht tells us as he tries to comfort his tearful wife. "I hate to leave you. Hate for all of us to leave you. But you'll be safer here," he says. "We must trust in the mercy of the enemy."

Trust in the mercy of the enemy?

In the darkness of two A.M., I hold tightly to Jed's hand as we watch General Milroy and his command flee the fort—men on horses, men on mules, men driving wagons, men marching. Soldiers marching. Thousands of soldiers marching—leaving all the women, children and the badly wounded behind.

Leaving Mrs. Houseknecht, the Billy-Bobs, Jed and me, behind.

FORTY A CONFEDERATE FLAG

now waves at us from that tall pole where General Milroy once kept watch. The flag's the same color as our great flag of the Union—red, white and blue. Only the Confederate one is mostly white with a red square in the upper left corner holding two crossed blue bars. On these bars are thirteen stars that stand for the eleven states of the Confederacy and for the secession governments in Kentucky and Missouri, too. Private Majer told me so. He's a *kind* Rebel guard (unlike a certain Corporal Nelson). *Kind* Private Majer goes with me when I leave the fort to gather firewood so that Mrs. Houseknecht can cook and do her laundry. Life must go on.

The flag that waves above the fort—newly named *Fort Jackson*—was raised three days ago in a huge ceremony attended by General Ewell, head of the Second Corps of the Army of Northern Virginia. As the flag was hoisted, this is what the triumphant men in gray sang while Private Majer's little dog, Flapjack, did somersaults in the air and five hundred of us weary Yankee prisoners (civilians and captured Union soldiers, too) looked on:

> We are a band of brothers, and native to the soil,
> Fighting for our Liberty, with treasure, blood and
>   toil;
> And when our rights were threatened, the cry rose
>   near and far,
> Hurrah for the Bonnie Blue Flag that bears a
>   single star!
> Hurrah! Hurrah! For Southern rights Hurrah!
> Hurrah for the Bonnie Blue Flag that bears a
>   single star.

I wondered why the troops were hurrahing a flag with a single star when the one flying above the fort clearly held thirteen? When I asked Private Majer about this, he couldn't answer. Joshua McDowell could have. "The Bonnie Blue Flag" was his favorite song. I wonder if he ever learned "The Battle Hymn of the Republic"?

Each day, I softly hum "The Battle Hymn" for courage as I sadly watch Rebel guards march groups of our wounded Union soldiers out of Fort Jackson to a foul prison for enlisted men located in Richmond—Belle Isle. Corporal Nelson tells me it's an island in the middle of the James River with no shelter from the hot June sun but two cherry trees. Six thousand Federal prisoners have already been confined there. If I don't stop complaining about the food at *Fort Jackson*, Corporal Nelson says he'll personally see I'm marched off to Belle Isle, too.

That Corporal Nelson is a blowhard. He can't march me off to Belle Isle! I'm a civilian. I'm Mrs. House-knecht's son. Jed and I are officially registered with the Confederate Army as Jed and Adam Houseknecht, prisoners of war, and Chaplain Eberhart looks out for us. The Rebels put him in charge of the civilian prisoners at Fort Jackson (and some wounded Union soldiers still in town). Over the past five days of our imprisonment, Jed and I have seen Chaplain Eberhart several times. We always ask if he's had news of Pa.

The chaplain hasn't.

I wonder why Mrs. McDowell hasn't found a way to contact us about him? She must know Jed and I are here. Fort Jackson is just outside Winchester where her prayer group meets. They'd know the conquering Rebels took civilian prisoners. I keep hoping Mrs. McDowell will march on Fort Jackson, demand our freedom and take us to Pa. Each day, I hope to see her bustle through the main gate and put our Rebel captors in their place.

She hasn't.

As for Chaplain McCabe? He's in town, caring for wounded soldiers and looking after the comfort of some Union officers' wives and daughters—seventeen in all. General Milroy left them behind, too. This morning, Chaplain McCabe sent Jed and me his regards via Chaplain Eberhart. These regards include the four things Chaplain McCabe told us earlier: "Cheer up, be hopeful and look on the bright side. All will be well."

My brother and I do need to cheer ourselves up. Yesterday, Corporal Nelson told us Lee crossed the Potomac. Lee plans to inflict a crushing defeat on us Yanks in our own backyard. Jed and I both know Lee will never do that. The Union Army will beat him back! Still, we are a little worried. To keep us ever hopeful, we've made up a list of things that, over our five days as prisoners of war at Fort Jackson, we think make up the bright side of life:

1. Unlike crowded Belle Isle, the fort is quite roomy. The younger children—including Jed and the Billy-Bobs—have room to chase Flapjack. In the cool of the evening, Private Majer's little dog loves to play "keep away." Usually, what Flapjack's trying to keep away is a pair of the Billy-Bobs' undershorts, which he has stolen from Mrs. Houseknecht's laundry pile.

2. The Rebels aren't sure how to handle women and children as prisoners of war; they don't know what to do with us or where to send us. Until they decide our fate, they pretty much let us do as we please within the confines of the fort. This is provided we don't sing songs such as "We Are Coming, Father Abraham," which Jed did once. Corporal Nelson overheard Jed and threatened to lock him up in solitary confinement if he ever sang that song again. Corporal Nelson likes to frighten us and I hate him for it.

3. Flapjack. Private Majer's brown and white spotted dog can do more tricks than any dog Jed and I have ever met. Not only can Flapjack do somersaults in the air to "The Bonnie Blue Flag," but he walks on his hind legs, drills with the men, stands at attention during inspection, loves everyone and, of course, keeps us all entertained by playing "keep away."

4. Finally, there is Private Majer, Flapjack's owner and trainer. Jed and I both like Private Majer. He is nineteen

years old. He loves farms and dogs, and he's from Balti-more, Maryland, which is not that far from our home in Pennsylvania. Once the war is over (a war Jed and I still keep telling ourselves the North will win), Private Majer can join us for dinner at Mister Eli's oyster bar!

5. Jed thought number four would be the end, but I had to add this. Everyone here thinks I'm a boy—includ-ing Private Majer, Chaplain Eberhart and Corporal Nel-son. I've completely transformed myself—I am Adam. When I complain to Corporal Nelson about the rotten food we're given, he yells at me: "Keep your trap shut or you'll find yourself being marched off to Belle Isle with the men!"

6. I thought that number five would be the end of the bright side, but Jed insisted we include this next part. Jed has found someone he can talk to about niter and that someone is none other than Private Majer himself! It seems that niter is not only found in caves, but you can also make it. Which is what the Confederate Army had to do, seeing as how they were faced with a shortage of niter and, as we all know, niter is needed, along with sulphur and charcoal, to make gunpowder.

According to Private Majer, this is how you can make niter for yourself. First, have everybody in your town save the urine in their chamber pots. Have them dump their urine into barrels you pass round. Now hold on to this because you're going to need it later. Dig a trench and fill it with animal carcasses, manure and vegetable scraps. Pour stagnant water over this and then add that urine you've collected. After decomposing for eighteen months, shovel this compost into hoppers and thoroughly leach it with water. You'll end up with several ounces of niter to the cubic foot.

Jed thinks this is the most fascinating and useful fact he's learned since he went off to see the elephant. For him, it is, perhaps, the brightest side of life at Fort Jackson. Now that I'm Adam Houseknecht, I would have to agree the whole thing's fascinating, but it's not all that useful or bright. It takes too much work.

And now for the darkest side of life here. It's so dark all of the bright things Jed and I listed earlier can't dispel it. After ruminating over our fate for five days, the Rebel Army has finally decided what to do with its civilian prisoners. Corporal Nelson says the decision came about in retaliation for something General Milroy did to the citizens of Winchester. During his six-month stay, General Milroy evicted several Southern families (not just the Logans) from their homes. General Milroy marched them through Winchester and dumped them alongside the road without food or shelter. If the Union Army can do this to defenseless civilians, why can't the Rebel Army do the same?

However, the Rebel Army has a heart, Corporal Nelson says. It doesn't want to abandon civilians to a wilderness where they can be set upon by wolves and thieves and marching armies. It wants to put all of us Yankee women and children, including the officers' wives and daughters, in a safe place. And where would that place be? A prison so deep in the heart of the Confederacy, Jed and I may never see our pa or the North again—

Castle Thunder.

FORTY ONE

WHEN ROSCOE FIRST told me about Castle Thunder, I had imagined the prison to be something out of Thumbelina country—a massive stone fortress in which an evil toad-king might live with his black dog, Nero. In one of the stone towers would be a window where a captured princess could call out to her prince with the aquiline nose. He'd come dashing up on his gray horse. He'd storm the prison walls and rescue the princess and her little brother, too.

However, after traveling for four days on foot and by rail to get to this prison, and having put fairy tales behind me, I know this sort of thing could never happen. For one thing, the real Castle Thunder Jed and I approach is nothing but three brick buildings attached together by a high board fence. For another, there is no such thing as that kind of prince.

The prison, fronting Cary Street, stands among ugly warehouses and factories spread out along the James River on the eastern end of the Confederate capital of Richmond. One of the guards who herds our group toward the prison tells us the main building, the middle one up ahead, is an ancient tobacco factory. See that platform hanging over the front door where two soldiers stand guard? That platform was used for drying tobacco. From a barred window next to this platform, a hoarse voice cries out, "Look at this, boys! Fresh fish and there's women, too!"

"What does fresh fish mean?" Jed stops to ask Chaplain Eberhart. He's accompanying us to Castle Thunder. Once he sees we're *comfortably settled,* he'll be marched on to Libby Prison, which is for Federal officers and is down the street. Chaplain Eberhart says, "It means new prisoners, Jed."

"Fresh prisoners for the men to rob and beat." Corporal Nelson pokes his rifle butt into my little brother's ribs. "Keep moving."

I draw Jed close to me. Why couldn't Private Majer have come with us instead of Corporal Nelson? Private Majer wouldn't prod Jed with a rifle. Private Majer wouldn't have whacked me in the head with a rifle butt the way Corporal Nelson did four days ago.

We were being marched south through Winchester on our way to Richmond and all I did was call out to Uncle Butler. I saw him in the crowds lining the streets and I called out—"Uncle Butler! Tell my pa—" That was all I got out. I knew nothing more until I awoke in one of the wagons the Rebels had brought along to transport the small and weak. Jed, in the wagon with me, cradled my aching head in his lap.

"Don't you worry, Adam," Jed told me. "Uncle Butler will tell Pa where we're off to. Our pa will find us. He'll beat up that Corporal Nelson and save us from the Rebel Army, too." Jed said this even though he's already told me he thinks Mrs. McDowell has turned Pa over to General Lee. Jed was trying to show me the bright side and cheer me up, I know. I also know Mrs. McDowell would never turn Pa over to the Rebels. She'd die first. Still, we're too far south for Pa or anyone else to rescue us now.

We must save ourselves.

I grip Jed's hand tightly as the pushy guards herd our group of women and children, and Chaplain Eberhart, through a heavy stained door and into the steamy, dark, evil-smelling prison. A guard calls out to someone down the long hall ahead, "More fresh fish."

"Cheeky boy," Mary, the youngest and prettiest of the laundry women, says. "We're no fish. We're Yankee ladies." The guard stares boldly at her and says, "You're no lady."

But she is. Mary is the loveliest of ladies with rose red cheeks and dark hair, long and curly the way mine used to be. I hold out my arm to Mary and my shoulder bumps by accident against the guard's chest. "Watch where you're going!" he yells at me so loudly, I jump.

With Jed holding my one hand and Mary taking the other, we three walk bravely abreast down the long hot dingy hallway with floorboards stained the color of barnyard mud. The hall smells of dirty laundry and something else so foul smelling, I'm afraid to figure out what it might be.

In a small hot room that has what looks like a bloodied thumbprint on the dirty white-washed wall next to the single barred window, we anxiously wait for the prison warden to tell us where we are to go next. Gray-haired Alice, who recites Psalm 46 when she's scared, whispers to me, "Pray hard for mercy. We don't want the men's lockup. I'm told the riffraff in there will eat us alive."

"You don't want the gallows, neither," Corporal Nelson says. He's so close I can smell his breath. His breath smells evil. "The gallows is what you get if you don't act right in here. Or a bullet through the heart."

He didn't have to tell us that!

A black-bearded man wearing a black shirt and tightly fitted black pants swaggers into the room where we've been herded together, scared as rabbits. The man has two pistols in holsters strapped to his sides and he wears a silver-handled sword in a scabbard. He's putting on a bully show to frighten us even more than we are now. We're just women and children! A huge black dog trots by his side. "Look at that dog!" a Billy-Bob whispers.

"That must be Nero, the prison warden's dog," I hear Jed whisper back. *Nero!* Jed says, "My friend Roscoe told me if you breathe too hard, Nero will bite off your toes."

"Mama, that dog bites off little boys' toes!" a Billy-Bob shouts. He tries to climb up his mother's skirt and the other Billy-Bob starts screaming, "Bad dog! Bad dog!"

"Pipe down, you two." Corporal Nelson shoves his gun butt against a Billy-Bob and the little boy tumbles backward onto the dirty floor.

"Pick on someone your own size," I find myself yelling at Corporal Nelson. I've had enough of him! Enough of all of this! I push his rifle to one side. He grabs the barrel end with one hand and the stock with the other. He flattens the gun against my chest and shoves me into Mrs. Houseknecht! I shove back. Corporal Nelson stumbles backward into the man in black while I yell into the corporal's reddening face, "You ugly June bug!"

"What did you call me?" he says.

"He called you a June bug!" Pretty Mary laughs.

"That's because he is one." Looking from Corporal Nelson to the man in black, I say, "Him and everyone else here who bullies defenseless people and takes away their freedom."

"You don't deserve freedom." Corporal Nelson pulls the gun toward his chest, then slams it back at me. Chaplain Eberhart places his hand on Corporal Nelson's shoulder. Chaplain Eberhart says, "Ease up on the boy."

Corporal Nelson lowers his rifle and I feel a hand on my shoulder now. *The man in black.* His fingers locate that tender hollow between my shoulder and collarbone and dig in. I feel their warning—don't move or we'll dig harder. I become as still as stone. The huge black dog sits himself down next to my right foot.

With his hand on my shoulder, the man in black tells us all that he is the prison warden—Captain Alexander. Oh no. He's the one Roscoe said hangs up prisoners by their thumbs and then calls for the rats to eat off their toes! *Captain Alexander* welcomes us to Castle Thunder. He says once his guards have searched and registered us, they'll escort us to Whitlock's Warehouse—reserved for women, children and colored folk. "It's clean and airy. You'll be comfortable.

"But I brook no insurrection in my prison. None whatsoever." Captain Alexander squeezes my shoulder. "This fellow here has already shown he's too much of a rabble-rouser to be housed with women. He's too old anyway.

"He belongs with the men."

I belong with the men?

"But that rabble-rouser's my brother!" loyal Jed calls out. "If he belongs in the men's lockup, so do I!"

"May as well throw me—along with my Billy-Bobs—in there, too," Mrs. Houseknecht says stoutly. "Adam's my own dear son."

"He's my sweetheart!" Pretty Mary says.

"You'll be locked up with cutthroats and thieves," Captain Alexander says to my loyal *kin,* and to my sweetheart. "They'll think nothing of beating you to a pulp and then robbing you blind. Are you sure you want to risk that to be with him?"

Jed nods. Mrs. Houseknecht and Mary nod. Oh no. The Billy-Bobs are nodding their heads, too.

I can't let this happen!

"Captain Alexander," I say. "I am not a him."

"What's that?" He turns me so that I face him. He's holding his head at a funny angle. He must be hard of hearing. I repeat a little louder, "I may be a rabble-rouser but I am not a him."

"I don't think I heard you right," he says.

"I AM NOT A HIM!" I say it out loud in front of everyone who thought I was.

"I am Anna Sunday."

FORTY TWO

THE GOOD THING ABOUT admitting who I am at Castle Thunder is that I can be myself and answer to my true name—Anna. When the guards are about to take away Chaplain Eberhart to Libby Prison, I can thank the chaplain who tried to stop Corporal Nelson from hurting me and lightly kiss the chaplain's cheek—*goodbye*. And, when the prison guard searches me and finds my special rock (which, even though it was given to me by someone I can hardly bear to think of, I can't seem to give up), I can plead with him to let me keep it and he does.

The bad thing is, Mrs. Houseknecht is upset. "Why didn't you tell me?" she says. And Captain Alexander, after his guards have escorted us to a squalid room that's our lockup (it has bars on the window and only one window at that), orders me to wear a dress! The homespun dress he gives me is ugly and smells of someone else's perspiration. I tell him in what I think is a haughty tone, "I prefer to wear trousers."

"A lady wears a dress," he says.

"Then I am no lady." His nostrils flare up when I say this. I don't care. I want to wear trousers. In them, I've done all sorts of things I never thought I could. In trousers, I . . . feel free. It's likely the only freedom I'll ever get in this steaming hot room with thirty of us crammed inside it like sardines in a can.

"You never should have left home. A woman's place is in the home!" Captain Alexander says, not only to me, but also to the others, all fanning their faces in the late June heat.

"Then let her go home!" Mary shouts. Others take up the cry—"We are ladies! We don't belong in this infernal prison! We want to go home!"

"Well you can't. There's a war going on. We've got the North in a state of panic." That wicked Captain Alexander, wearing all his guns and a sword, too, doesn't elaborate on this. He just jingles his set of prison keys and smiles to himself.

Pox on him!

A day in prison passes all too slowly when you're hot and bored and worried about the North. It's too hot and crowded in here! All I have is a six by two foot space of hard floor to lie on with my head propped on a soiled blanket a prison guard gave me! On my first full afternoon here, the Billy-Bobs get sick from the heat and throw up their noon meal of bacon soup all over my sleeping space. No matter how hard I scrub the floor, I can't get rid of the sour scent.

My relief is to stand at the corner window and breathe in the fresh air. Today, June 26, my second day in prison, I watch from the window as Rebel guards herd Chaplain

McCabe, with the seventeen officers' wives and daughters left behind by General Milroy, into Castle Thunder. An hour later, guards escort Chaplain McCabe down the street to Libby Prison. I will the wind to whisper in the chaplain's ear what I am trying hard to believe myself— "All will be well." I already know I dare not shout the words to him. I'd get shot.

Jed and I stand at the window every chance we get. Through the bars, we watch life go by in the world outside while the wind off the James River fans our faces and we try to ignore the guards below us tramping back and forth. I long to be where I can walk freely without stumbling over someone. And be alone when I please in a place that smells nice. I want to go home.

"One day, we'll be out of here," Jed says.

"Yes we will but until we do, we must remember what Pa says—'Hot fires make strong bricks.' "

"I miss our pa," Jed says. I miss Pa, too. I miss him so much my heart aches.

Everyone likes standing at the window, so we all must take turns. As the days pass, one hot day slowly dragging itself into the next, we hear newspaper boys from the street below shouting out headlines. On our *sixth* morning in prison, a newsboy shouts up at Jed and me: "General Lee's army has invaded Pennsylvania!"

"I can't believe it." Jed looks up at me.

"I can't believe it, either, Jed." Hot tears sting my eyes. The Union Army was supposed to stop Lee! Oh I can't bear to think of war coming to my backyard! There's Cousin Ezekiel! To say nothing of Lauden Honor and our dog, Anarchy.

It's now midafternoon and no one shouts out head-lines from the street below. It's too hot. Through the win-dow, I can just see over the roofs of the old factories across the street, to the James River, shimmering in the heat. Beyond it are more factories and then broad fields and rolling hills. A hawk—just a speck in the horizon—soars above a bright green field.

I grip the window bars and shake them. I want to go home. Even if war's there, I want to go home.

"Anna, we want to hear the Thumbelina story," Jed calls over to me. Jed's trying to be a strong brick. For the past hour he and the other children have been racing lice in Mrs. Houseknecht's old frying pan. You wouldn't think you could race such tiny creatures, but you can.

"You don't want to hear that silly 'Thumbelina,' " I call over the rows of women lined up on the floor, trying to nap in the afternoon heat.

"Yes we do," Jed says. "But we don't want the whole story. Just the part where Thumbelina's held prisoner by the field mouse and that mole who wants to marry her and keep her shut up in the dark forever. We want to hear how the swallow, after Thumbelina saves his life, flies her to freedom. We want a happy ending, Anna."

I want a happy ending, too. But I don't feel like telling stories.

"Come on, Anna!" Jed shouts.

"Shush, Jed. You'll wake everyone up." I sit next to him to keep him quiet and the other children crowd around me. Jed says, "I'll start. Once there was this girl who meets a swallow, dying in the mud."

"You can't start there. People need the whole Thumbelina story to appreciate the swallow part." I don't want to tell this story.

"Just the swallow part," Jed says.

"I want the whole thing," says red-cheeked Penelope. "Me, too," says Elisabeth with strubly hair. Everyone except for Jed and the Billy-Bobs takes up the cry, "The whole story! The whole story, Anna!"

Jed sighs loudly. I sigh loudly, reluctant to begin. But once I do and I move into Thumbelina's many adventures, rutchety Jed grows quiet and I become caught up in them, too. This is because, having lived as a boy for quite some time, I find myself changing the story as I go along. I substitute the word *brave* for *pretty*. *Brave* Thumbelina doesn't cry so much when things go wrong. When an ugly June bug tries to fly off with her, *brave* Thumbelina stands up for herself; she puts up a fight. The Billy-Bobs and Jed like this part so much they stop me so they can add to it:

"Thumbelina pops that June bug on the head," a Billy-Bob says.

"She bites off his pincers!" says the other.

"What's a June bug?" Penelope asks.

"It's an ugly creature who's mean to others. Corporal Nelson is a June bug," I say.

"Thumbelina dumps *that* ugly June bug down the latrine where he belongs!" Jed says.

This starts everybody talking about the smelly latrines—located outside in the prison yard. The latrines smell worse than rotten eggs broken over a pile of old dead rats. Jed says we should dump all June bugs, ugly toads, hungry rats and bacon soup down the latrines. "We'll let it all settle there for eighteen months and, by the end, we'll have niter," Jed says. "We'll mix the niter with charcoal and sulphur and that'll make gunpowder."

"We'll blow the smelly latrines sky-high!" a Billy-Bob yells, awakening several women. They tell us to "Hush," before turning over on their lice-ridden mats to go back to their naps. Pretty Mary, who's been listening to the story, helps me settle the children down so that I can continue. Mary wants to know what happens after the fight with the June bug. And does Thumbelina, once she's stuck in the dark hole with the field mouse and the mole who wants to marry her, ever escape?

Well, of course she does. And brave Thumbelina ends up riding the swallow through the sunlit sky to a bright country that smells of oranges. Here, and it hurts for me to say this next part, she meets the prince with the aquiline nose who asks her to be his wife. At this very point, a gust of wind blows through our one window. From clear across the room, the wind fans the damp hair on the back of my neck.

I turn to feel that wind on my face and that's when I hear a trumpet. The full notes of a trumpet ride the breeze coming through the window. And what is that far-off trumpet playing, from somewhere across the James River where there are fields where hawks soar free? A song that brought Samson the courage to cross the treacherous Potomac on a ferryboat—"The Battle Hymn of the Republic"!

Could this be Joshua playing the trumpet? Who else would have a fancy trumpet that can play such glorious tunes? Joshua's telling me he figured out the song to raise Samson off his hindquarters! That Samson's with Pa now!

"Who'd play our 'Battle Hymn' in the heart of the Confederacy?" Mary says as we all rush to the window. Guards are swarming out of Castle Thunder and onto the cobbled street below. Guards shout—"Stop that noise! Stop it now!"—as if their words could be carried clear across the river and over factory buildings to the fields of glory that lie beyond—*Glory! Glory hallelujah!*

"Must be some foolhardy Yankee sympathizer protesting Lee's invasion of Pennsylvania," Mary says.

"Or a Rebel boy I once knew." It *could* be Joshua.

"That's not Joshua!" Jed shouts in my ear.

"Uncle Butler could have told him we were here," I say. The distant notes wash over me. Joshua plays slowly and with such majesty. I have never heard him play so well.

"That's not Joshua," Jed repeats. "It's impossible," Jed says. "No boy with kin in Jackson's old brigade would play 'The Battle Hymn of the Republic' in Richmond, the Rebel capital! Which also happens to be one hundred and fifty miles from his home. It's a foolhardy Yankee sympathizer, Anna. You have my word on it," Jed says.

"Well Jed," I say. *"That* word isn't worth a fart in a whirlwind! Because you know what? I believe in impossibilities! Fairy tales can come true!" That *could* be Joshua out there. And if it isn't? Still, it's not someone foolhardy. It's someone very brave who's reminding me I'm a part of something far bigger than I am. And even though I am in prison, Lee's invaded Pennsylvania and I may never see my home again, I must keep marching resolutely onward—*All will be well.*

FORTY THREE

WHOEVER PLAYED "The Battle Hymn of the Republic" in the heart of Dixie has struck a note of terror in the minds of our Rebel captors. It has told them that the end of the world is coming, they'd better make restitution for all their sins. Why else would they be releasing all forty-seven of us Yankee women and children from Castle Thunder on this, the sunlit morning of the very next day?

Jed claims it's because a guard overheard his plans to make gunpowder. Mary says it's because the Rebel Army finally realized we're ladies. You don't lock up ladies in a prison reserved for the scum of the earth. I insist it was the "Battle Hymn."

It's not until we are on a flag of truce boat steaming down the James River to the Union stronghold, Fortress Monroe, that we learn the true reason for our release—three hundred Rebel women. The U.S. Secretary of War, Edwin Stanton, held up the transportation of three hundred Rebel women from Annapolis, Maryland, to their homes in Dixie until he knew for certain the forty-seven

Yankee women and children held at Castle Thunder for six days had been released from captivity and were safe. At the same time we'd be steaming north to freedom, the Rebel women would be steaming south.

It's when we are on board a second boat and headed up the Chesapeake Bay toward a place where prisoners of war are exchanged—Camp Parole in Annapolis, Maryland—that I actually see these Rebel women. They crowd the deck of an approaching steamboat. It is dusk. The sun, about to sink below the horizon, glints off the Chesapeake's choppy waves.

I learn through our boat captain that these Rebel women had been visiting with Yankee relatives up north until the panic caused by Lee's advancing army made them pack their carpetbags. I realize with a start that these women are much like Jed and me—crossing boundary lines to be with kin.

I want to bring these women the same note of hope the playing of the "Battle Hymn" brought me! I run to the stern of our boat and I lean over the railing. As my boat steams north and theirs steams south, I sing out a line from what I think must be their favorite song— "Hurrah for the Bonnie Blue Flag that bears a single star."

Several women all in black wave their white handkerchiefs back.

At Camp Parole, Jed and I register much as we did at Fort Jackson and Castle Thunder. Only this time, we face a soldier in Union blue instead of Confederate gray. This time I give my true name right off: "Anna Sunday." Of course, the soldier gives me a peculiar look. Of course, he questions my wearing trousers and why were Jed and I at Winchester anyway?

"To save our wounded pa," I say.

"His name is Private Abraham Sunday," Jed says.

"And where is Private Sunday?" the soldier asks.

"We don't know." I'm not about to tell him my pa's staying with the feistiest Rebel lady you ever did meet. One day, she'll bring him—and Glory—home. She will!

"Who do we notify of your release?" the soldier asks.

"Cousin Ezekiel?" Jed looks over at me.

"I don't think so, Jed. He'd get too confused." I turn to the soldier. "You'll have to telegram our neighbor Miss Bemis. She'll tell our cousin."

"Where does this Miss Bemis live?" the soldier asks.

"New Oxford, Pennsylvania." At his blank look I explain that it's seven miles north of Hanover and between York and Gettysburg.

"*Gettysburg?*" The soldier rubs his temples. "A battle's going on there. Didn't you know? Our captain says whatever happens at Gettysburg could decide the outcome of the war."

"But it's such a little town." I've heard it called a spit in the road. "Why are they fighting there?"

"Word has it Rebs and Yanks alike had gone to Gettysburg looking for shoes." The soldier shakes his head. "Can you beat that? War coming to a little market town—all for the want of shoes."

Summer wheat has turned the Pennsylvania countryside to gold. It's Tuesday, July 7, and the train that Jed and I ride on passes field after field of burning gold, bright in the hot July sun. We boarded the train yesterday at the crowded Baltimore train station. The train will drop us off at New Oxford on its way to Gettysburg.

We ride in an open train car. It's just a box on wheels, added to make room for the hundreds of people going to the battlefield to search for missing kin, tend to the wounded and bury the dead. The battle has ended in a Union victory. Newspapers call it—"A Great Victory!" I'm relieved our soldiers beat back Lee, but still, I wouldn't call it a great victory. There've been up to fifty thousand casualties! A surgeon traveling with us says there are so many wounded soldiers from both sides they fill just about every building in Gettysburg—including warehouses and barns.

I'm almost afraid to go home.

Jed and I stare out at the fields we pass. Cows, ignoring our noisy train, graze peacefully, bronze against the deep green grass. Clover and Queen Anne's lace are all in bloom. It makes it hard to believe a bloody battle has been fought just miles from here. In the distance ahead stands an old barn with white hex signs painted on it. As we draw closer, I see tulips painted within the white outlines of circles. I've never seen tulips painted on barns—only stars.

Pa loved tulips.

"Why did that farmer paint tulips on his barn?" Jed wonders aloud.

"So brave Thumbelinas can pop out of them," I say.

"That's not true," Jed says.

"It's as true as fairy tales." There must be a certain truth to fairy tales. Why else would we tell them?

"Know what my fairy tale would be?" Jed says. "That Samson would be at the New Oxford train station, hitched to Cousin Ezekiel's old wagon. And who should be in that wagon? Cousin Ezekiel and Pa."

"I wish that, too." Oh I *do* wish that. That would make me the happiest girl alive! But it could never happen.

I must be brave.

When our train pulls into New Oxford, there isn't even a wagon waiting for us. There's just an old black buggy parked in the back lot. We don't own a buggy and neither does Miss Bemis. However, the horse hitched to it does look familiar—big and gray. Something seems to be perched on the horse's head. Is that Miss Pete? No. It can't be. It's probably just a hat.

FORTY FOUR

OUR TRAIN STEAMS TO a stop in front of New Oxford's redbrick station and so I don't see the horse anymore. Just a small gray-haired man standing at the ticket window. A hot sad ache fills my throat. In the three months we've been gone, something must have happened to Cousin Ezekiel and Miss Bemis, too.

War kills off everything.

"Maybe Miss Bemis never got the telegram," Jed says.

"That must be it, Jed." I need to be brave for my little brother. The surgeon in our train car said it will take a month of rain to wash the blood of slain soldiers off our Pennsylvania soil. Some of that blood must belong to civilians. I feel as if my heart will break.

A porter helps Jed and me out of our open boxcar. We say goodbye to the surgeon and he tells us, "God bless." I throw my bedroll over my shoulder the way a boy would do. Jed throws his bedroll over his. We move resolutely forward the way Mrs. McDowell's Potawatomi Indians once did—placing one foot in front of the other. And now, that small man with iron gray hair hurries toward us. *What does he want?*

He says, "Is that you, Jed Sunday? Adam Sunday, is that you?" He looks like a dandy in that fancy dark frock coat he has on. And in all this heat! Is he a friend of Cousin Ezekiel's? How does this little man know my boy's name?

"I've been waiting here for hours!" he says rather sharply to us for someone we don't know. Or do we? He looks familiar. I stare hard at the little man. He stares hard back. *He has Mrs. McDowell's pale green eyes.*

"Someone had to bring your father home," she says as Jed and I stand there stunned. She wears black broadcloth pants, black frock coat, a white shirt and a black bow tie. She's cut off her hair. She's disguised herself as a man! "You don't think I'd let your father travel here on his own, now do you? Not at a time like this!" She fiddles with her shirt collar. *She's wearing trousers just like me.* She says, "With war going on, getting your father home required the wits of Reb and Yank alike.

"Where have you been? Your train's over eight hours late! I've been worried to a frazzle!" she says.

"We were held prisoner at Fort Jackson and you never came to save us." I swallow to keep the tears away. I know this is not what she's asking for, but it's been on my mind.

"There were no Sundays registered at Fort Jackson," she says. "I checked the rolls myself."

"There were Houseknechts. Jed and Adam Houseknecht," Jed says and she says, "Well how was I to know that?"

"I don't know." Jed kicks at the dust. Jed says, "Where's our pa?"

"I made him go home. To *your* home," she adds. "He was plumb worn out from waiting for you in all this heat."

"Is that Samson hitched to the buggy out back?" Jed says.

"You don't think it would be one of my horses now do you? Your Union Army stole all my horses," she calls after Jed, who's taken off for Samson at a run. I want to run to Samson, too. But there's Mrs. McDowell and she's dressed in trousers. She places her hand on my arm. Her green eyes look so deeply, so lovingly into mine. She says, "How are you, Adam Sunday?"

"You can call me Anna now, Mrs. McDowell. I have decided to be Anna even in trousers. I like wearing trousers. I might stay in trousers. There's a certain freedom in wearing them. Don't you think? In hard times, you discover all sorts of surprising things about yourself in them." As the words pour out of me, Mrs. McDowell's eyes swell with tears. She laughs as she wipes these tears away.

"Where's Cousin Ezekiel?" He's the one who insisted I wear trousers from the start!

"That man is so excited! And do you know why?" Mrs. McDowell is smiling now. "It seems a certain pig named Charity is in labor. Your cousin is with Miss Bemis right now to help that pig give birth.

"Though I would think a pig perfectly capable of giving birth on her own," she says as we hurry to the buggy. Pa's home! And piglets are coming.

"And Joshua. Where is he?" I ask.

"With Uncle Butler and Miss Adelaide, I should

think. Although knowing that fool boy, he could be most anyplace. He said to tell you how sorry he is. He didn't mean to keep Samson for so long. He . . . encountered certain difficulties . . ."

I'm sure he did! And here's our Samson now with that little Rebel Miss Pete perched on his head! Samson's dark eyes are glazed over with delight; Jed's scratching Samson's itchy spot. I join Jed in scratching and the old horse lifts his head. He curls his upper lip inside out. At the same time, Jed and I shout, "Praise the Lord, Samson!"

Samson lets out a whinny that praises the Lord from New Oxford clear on down to wherever Joshua may be.

In the buggy, Mrs. McDowell hands me the reins. With her on one side of me, Jed on the other and Miss Pete nestled in Jed's lap because Samson's glorious whinny has startled her off his head, I shout, "Love thy neighbor, Samson!" And our beautiful old Bible horse moves out, his big gray hooves churning up our reddish-brown dust.

New Oxford, Pennsylvania
July 10, 1863

Dear Joshua,

I must tell you about Miss Bemis's pet pig Charity. Our neighbor's pig, with our Lauden Honor as proud father, gave birth to nine piglets, which, as we all know, is a sure sign of good things to come as nine is a multiple of three as in Father, Son and Holy Ghost. I think this means this cruel war, which causes men to lose their limbs and pits friend against friend, is soon coming to an end.

Miss Bemis gave one piglet to Cousin Ezekiel and another to your grandmother who's now called Angus. She'll stay Angus until us Sundays can get her safely back through the Union lines. Angus has named her black and white piglet Merciful Redemption.

Joshua, we all think Angus has more than redeemed herself by bringing our pa safely home to Pennsylvania. And to think she put on trousers to do it! She's brave and a little bossy, too. Already, she's laid down house rules for us Sundays to follow.

Your grandmother told me you had difficulties with Samson. That he wandered off and after almost a week you found him sitting on his hindquarters in a country church! Now Joshua, even I find that hard to believe. Someday you must tell me what really happened and I'll do the same for you. But for now, stay well. Don't let any pigs step on your feet and if you see Uncle Butler, tell him for me—

Root, hog, or die!

Love,
Anna

P.S. I still have the rock you gave me.

Author's Note

While Anna Sunday is a work of fiction, her journey was inspired by real-life accounts of Civil War women. For most women, when the Civil War began it seemed to be the domain of men and older boys. They were the ones who marched off to fight while the ladies were expected to remain at home. Alice Ready, from Tennessee, confessed in her diary, "I never before wished I was a man—now I feel so keenly my weakness and dependence. I cannot do or say anything—for fear it would be unbecoming in a young lady—How I should love to fight and even die for my country . . ."

As the Civil War ground on, many women were forced to buck the status quo. They discovered hidden talents and strengths within themselves as they took on jobs formerly reserved for men. They plowed and planted fields. They butchered livestock. They cut firewood. They provided safe havens for their families, often in the face of danger and despair. They kept guns and knew how to fire them.

Some women left home to be with the fighting armies. Women could be found at camps and on battlefields as laundresses, sutlers, wives, and daughters of the regiment. Kady Brownwell was named flag bearer for her husband's Rhode Island regiment. She is credited with saving lives when she bravely raised her Union flag through a hail of gun fire, thereby alerting Yankee soldiers mistakenly firing at her regiment—"we are not the enemy!"

Others served as nurses in makeshift hospitals and on hospital ships. Mary Ann Bickerdyke cared for men wounded in nineteen Civil War battles! Whenever her authority was challenged (many considered the nursing of ailing soldiers an unfit profession for the gentler sex), she would answer, "I have received my authority from the Lord God almighty; have you anything that ranks higher than that?"

And then there were those who put on trousers and disguised themselves as men. In Civil War times, this was a brave and revolutionary act. Sarah Morgan of Louisiana writes, "I have heard so many girls boast of having worn men's clothes; I wonder where they got the courage."

Sara Emma Edmonds, who became Franklin Thompson, set out in male clothes to prove she could "outwork, outshoot, and outride any boy." Sara learned to swim, hunt, fish, paddle a canoe, and row a boat. As Franklin Thompson, she became a Civil War soldier and spy. Loreta Velazquez disguised herself as a soldier to be with her husband and even recruited her own battalion! It is said she pushed her voice as low as it would go, put on a manly swagger, and even practiced spitting in the street. Mary Edwards Walker, in trousers and a man's coat, trained as a doctor and, during the Civil War, served as surgeon both on the field and in the hospital.

The list goes on. In stepping outside their prescribed roles, these women challenged the ancient beliefs concerning a woman's need for protection and "lack of aptitude" for what had formerly been considered male-only tasks. These Civil War women opened up the doors to a freedom we all benefit from today. Mrs. Mary Lee, known as a Rebel she-devil by the Union Army who occupied her hometown of Winchester, writes in 1863 (near the start of it all), "I find myself, every day, doing something I never did before."

Selected Bibliography

When writing historical novels, I begin by researching something specific, whether it be the kidnapping of a young girl during the French and Indian Wars (*I Am Regina*), the massacre of American patriots at the Bloody Rock during the American Revolution (*Moon of Two Dark Horses*), or, in the case of Anna Sunday, "The Battle Hymn of the Republic." As I research, one source leads me to another. There are twists and turns in the road in which I often make delightful and interesting discoveries. As my exploration of the past widens from the original incident, slowly but surely, a story is born. This selected bibliography reflects that exploration and the story.

FEDERAL AND STATE GOVERNMENT PUBLICATIONS

Bates, Samuel P. *History of Pennsylvania Volunteers, 1861–5.* vol. III. Harrisburg: The State Printer, 1870.

The War of the Rebellion: A Compilation of the Official Records of the Union and Confederate Armies, series II, vol. VI, pp. 62, 63, 69, 72–75. Washington: Government Printing Office, 1899.

MEMOIRS, MEMOIR COLLECTIONS, AND REMINISCENCES

Cavada, Lieutenant-Colonel F. F. *Libby Life: Experiences of a Prisoner of War in Richmond, Va., 1863–64.* Lanham, New York, London: University Press of America, 1983.

Colt, Margaretta Barton. *Defend the Valley: A Shenandoah Family in the Civil War.* New York: Crown Publishers, 1994.

Granger, Moses Moorhead. *The Official War Record of the 122nd Regiment of Ohio Volunteer Infantry from October 8, 1862, to June 26, 1865.* Zanesville, Ohio: George Lilienthal, printer, 1912.

Lee, Mrs. Hugh. *Diary,* March 1862–November 1865 (civilian) typescript, 891 leaves. The Archives Room, The Handley Regional Library, Winchester-Frederick County Historical Society.

McDonald, Cornelia Peake. *A Woman's Civil War: A Diary, with Reminiscences of the War, from March 1862.* Madison, Wisconsin: The University of Wisconsin Press, 1992.

Miller, Gettie (Margaretta). *Diary,* March 23, 1863–September 9, 1863 (civilian—thirteen years old), manuscript. The Archives Room, The

Handley Regional Library, Winchester-Frederick County Historical Society.

Prowell, George Reeser. *History of the Eighty-seventh Regiment, Pennsylvania Volunteers, prepared from official records, diaries, and other authentic sources of information,* by George R. Prowell, Pub. Under the auspices of the regimental association. York, Pennsylvania, Press of the York Daily, 1903.

Sperry, Kate. *Diary, Surrender? Never Surrender.* 1861– typescript, bound, 633 pages. The Archives Room, The Handley Regional Library, Winchester-Frederick County Historical Society.

The Winchester-Frederick County Historical Society. *Diaries, Letters, and Recollections of the War Between the States.* Winchester: The Winchester-Frederick County Historical Society, 1955.

PRIMARY SOURCES FOR THE TIME AND LIFESTYLES

Child, Mrs. *The American Frugal Housewife.* Twelfth Edition. Boston: Carter, Hendee and Co., 1833.

Child, Mrs. *The Family Nurse.* Boston: Charles J. Hendee, 1837.

Thomas, Robert B. *The (old) Farmer's Almanack, Calculated on a New and Improved Plan, for the Year of Our Lord 1863.* Boston: Swan, Brewer & Tileston, 1863.

JOURNALS AND ARTICLES

Chance, Mark. "Prelude to Invasion: Lee's Preparations and the Second Battle of Winchester." *The Gettysburg Magazine* no. 19: pp. 5–36.

Fordney, Chris. "A Town Embattled." *Civil War Times Illustrated* XXXIV, no. 6, February 1996: pp. 30–37, 70.

Holswoth, Jerry W. "Quiet Courage: The Story of Winchester, Virginia, in the Civil War." *Blue & Gray Magazine* XV, issue 2, December 1997: pp. 6–26, 47–54.

Maryniak, Benedict. " 'They Also Serve, Who . . .': Jonathan Haralson and the Selma Nitriary." *Civil War: The Magazine of the Civil War Society* IX, no. 5, September–October 1991: p. 34.

Spear, Donald P. "The Sutler in the Union Army." *Civil War History,* vol. 16, no. 2, pp. 121–138. Kent, Ohio: Kent State University Press, 1970.

Secondary Sources

Bakeless, Katherine L. *Glory, Hallelujah!: The Story of The Battle Hymn of the Republic*. Philadelphia & New York: J. B. Lippincott Co., 1944.

Billings, John D. *Hardtack and Coffee: Or the Unwritten Story of Army Life*. Boston: George M. Smith & Co., 1887.

Bristol, Frank M. *The Life of Chaplain McCabe: Bishop of the Methodist Epsicopal Church*. New York: Felming H. Revell, 1908.

Chang, Ina. *A Separate Battle: Women and the Civil War*. New York: Lodestar Books, 1991.

Delauter, Roger U., Jr. *Winchester in the Civil War*. Lynchburg, Va.: H. E. Howard, Inc., 1992.

Faust, Drew Gilpin. *Mothers of Invention: Women of the Slaveholding South in the American Civil War*. Chapel Hill: University of North Carolina Press, 1996.

Grunder, Charles S. *The Second Battle of Winchester June 12–15, 1863*. c. 1989, H. E. Howard, Inc.

Hall, Richard. *Patriots in Disguise: Women Warriors of the Civil War*. New York: Paragon House, 1993.

Heaps, Willard A., and Porter W. Heaps. *The Singing Sixties: The Spirit of Civil War Days Drawn from the Music of the Times*. Norman: University of Oklahoma Press, 1960.

King, Elaine, and William L. Zeigler, and Alvin H. Jones, *History of New Oxford*. New Oxford, Pennsylvania: 1977.

Klees, Fredric. *The Pennsylvania Dutch*. New York: The Macmillan Co., 1950.

Kuz, Julian E., M.D., and Bradley P. Bengtson, M.D. *Orthopaedic Injuries of the Civil War: An Atlas of Orthopaedic Injuries and Treatments During the Civil War*. Kennesaw, Georgia: Kennesaw Mountain Press, Inc., 1996.

Lord, Francis A. *Civil War Sutlers and Their Wares*. New York: Thomas Yoseloff, 1969.

McCutcheon, Marc. *The Writer's Guide to Everyday Life in the 1800s*. Cincinnati: Writer's Digest Books, 1993.

McPherson, James M. *For Cause & Comrades: Why Men Fought in the Civil War*. New York: Oxford University Press, 1997.

Miller, Francis Trevelyan, and Robert S. Lanier. *The Photographic History of the Civil War*, vols. 3 & 4, 7 & 8. New York: Thomas Yoseloff, 1957.

Nye, Wilbur Sturtevant, *Here Come the Rebels!* Baton Rouge: Louisiana State University Press, 1965.

Quarles, Garland R. *Occupied Winchester 1861–1865.* Winchester, Virginia: Winchester-Frederick County Historical Society, 1991.

Robertson, James, Jr., and the editors of Time-Life Books. *The Civil War: Tenting Tonight.* Alexandria, Virginia: Time-Life Books, 1984.

Varhola, Michael J. *Everyday Life During the Civil War: A Guide for Writers, Students and Historians.* Cincinnati: Writer's Digest Books, 1999.

Young, Agatha. *The Women and the Crisis: Women of the North in the Civil War.* New York: McDowell, Obolensky, 1959.

STORY REFERENCES

Andersen, Hans Christian. *Thumbelina and Other Stories,* illustrated by Joan Gallup. Philadelphia: Running Press, 1989.

WEBSITES

I visited numerous Civil War Web sites when researching this novel. The Douglas's Texas Battery, CSA site, was particularly helpful in figuring out how heavy artillery is fired. One of the most extraordinary sites I visited was: Valley of the Shadow: The Civil War as Seen by Franklin County, Pennsylvania, and Augusta County, Virginia: www.jefferson.village.virginia.edu/vshadow2.